WEDNESDAY'S CHILD

A remarkable and original debut from an exciting new voice in fiction.

Janet Roberts and her brother James are at the mercy of their father's foul mood swings, especially on Wednesdays, when he returns from the night shift, angry and red-eyed, but they can always lose themselves in Janet's stories, or go and visit their boozy Aunt Net. Then, in the course of one summer on their Oxford council estate, everything changes. A girl is murdered in the park near their house. James disappears, Aunt Net goes off the rails and Janet's mother is hospitalised. Janet is left alone, with only her quick wits and vivid imagination to help her through.

WEDNESDAY'S CHILD

WEDNESDAY'S CHILD

by

Eloise Millar

Magna Large Print Books
Long Preston, North Yorkshire,
BD23 4ND, England.

British Library Cataloguing in Publication Data.

Millar, Eloise
  Wednesday's child.

  A catalogue record of this book is
  available from the British Library

  ISBN   0-7505-2272-0

First published in Great Britain by Virago in 2004

Published in Large Print 2004 by arrangement with
Time Warner Books UK

Magna Large Print is an imprint of Library Magna Books Ltd.

Printed and bound in Great Britain by
T.J. (International) Ltd., Cornwall, PL28 8RW

For J & MB

Acknowledgements

I would like to thank my agent, David Riding, and editor, Antonia Hodgson. Thanks also to Martin, Fay, Betty, Benny, Will, Becky, Jules, Raj, TC, Esther E & Esther C, Ben S and Diana J. Most of all, thanks to Sam.

One

1

Monday was Mum's day of irritation, not his. They were her ironing days. She would lug her ironing board into the kitchen and plough, huffing and puffing, through piles of clothes, while steaming pots of dinner bubbled all around her. She seemed most vulnerable when she did her ironing. There was a look of distracted concentration on her face; occasional murmurs issued from under her breath, soft and rhythmic, like the incantations of a benign witch. She looked tiny, stooping over the nylon shirts, trousers, homemade cardigans, prematurely aged, as though her life had withered her away. There were large purple bags beneath her eyes and clumps of greasy psoriasis hung like snowflakes from her curly black hair. A cigarette always drooped from her mouth and the smoke swirled lazily above her head, floating up to the ceiling to disperse on the yellowing tiles.

'Get out of it,' she'd usually end up snapping as, flushed and bending double, she left off ironing to cough into a freshly pressed handkerchief. 'Always under my feet. Go on, bugger off to Net's. Go and see if she needs anything.'

That was another thing about Mum, her cough. It had been around for so long, for as long as I could remember, that I suspected the deep, phlegmatic rumbles to have permeated the very walls of our house. I sometimes liked to imagine future occupants when I lay awake at night – people a hundred years from now, waking up in the early hours and shaking, crying, just like they did in ghost stories: 'Was that you? I heard it again. Was that you, coughing like that?'

Aunty Annette's was ten doors down from us, 182, Cumberland Road. Cumberland Road was the longest street round our way. The houses ran along in blocks of ten – little three ups, two downs, with box-like layouts, rectangle gardens at the back and tiny serf-square lawns at the front. Aunty Net lived beside the Hornet Swatting Tree, a massive, curvy willow, a leftover from the old greenwood, because Blackbird Leys had been an ancient wood before it had ever been a council estate. We scaled the Hornet Swatting Tree through the summers, armed with makeshift clubs and salvaged bits of

16

wood. We made it our mission to exterminate the insects that buzzed around its fragrant branches, and its knotted crevices and silky leaves sheltered us from rain and sun no matter how badly we battered it.

Mum called Aunty Net's The Disgrace. Why Aunty Net had taken it upon herself to call it Field View, she said, she'd never know. Apart from the putting on of airs and graces, giving a bloody council house a name, apart from that, *Field View?* What view? You could view bugger all, the windows were so filthy.

To James and me, the house was a chaotic paradise. Aunty Net's ragbag bits and bobs cluttered and tumbled out of every corner. Rubbish oozed out of the dustbin and into the front garden, mingling with the bin liners, bicycles and old carpets that lined the pot-holed path. A single roller-skate lay entwined in long grasses, its one remaining wheel facing heaven, and Aunty Net's mangy tabby, Manilow, was usually sprawled over either the dustbin lid or the haphazard pile of red bricks that had been there ever since the time a local gang had taken it upon themselves to knock down half her front wall. She'd watched them from behind the kitchen curtains, but it was late at night and she had said that she was too afraid to go outside and chase them away, even though I could never picture her frightened, not Aunty Net.

Inside, the cupboards teemed with silverfish, which scuttled in and out of rusting, bursting cans and moulding apples. She never threw anything away and had only ever lost her children, whom she kept forgetting to feed. Social Services had taken them away one day.

'Hello, my little darlings!' Groping through the hallway, Aunty Net threw her skinny, scaling arms around us.

She ruffled our hair in turn, and puckered our cheeks with emaciated fingers that clicked over our faces like dry bones.

'Look at you!' she cried, her red eyes glowing. 'So grown-up and beautiful. I always forget. Where have you been the past few days? Did you forget your poor old aunty?'

'We came round yesterday,' I said, easing out of my cardigan, which was itchy in the summer heat, as I tried hard to ignore James wrinkling his nose – at the smell, I supposed – and making vomiting motions in the doorway behind her back. He stuck his fingers down his throat and lurched over, pretend heaving, straightening hastily when she twisted round to look at him. 'Yesterday. Don't you remember?'

She hardly ever listened. She probably didn't even hear us, just as nobody heard her. Bloody Loony Tune, our dad, Dick Roberts, called her: Two Sultanas Short Of A Fruit Cake, Round The Bend. I'm Ashamed To Be Seen With That Sister Of Yours was one of his favourite phrases. We loved her, despite it all, the scruffy woman who was always pleased to see us and didn't care if we messed up her filthy house. Aunty Net's was the only home we knew where decorum and punctuality were the last things you had to think about. On her bad days she didn't even know whether it was night or day.

'It's nice to have a bit of company,' she clucked, hovering over us. 'I get so lonely here sometimes, all by myself.'

The welcome dispensed with, she glanced casually towards the flimsy blue carrier bag, which hung by my side. Her smile reached her eyes when she saw the contours of the litre bottle knocking against my legs, swinging gently to and fro.

Aunty Net's medicine.

It was the reason she was so pleased to see us, the one thing she always remembered. And to be fair, we didn't mind, even though

19

we'd get into trouble if Mum or Nan found out, because the stuff did bring her a short length of clarity – although, it was true, you could never be quite sure which way it would go: there was always the danger it would send her to the other extreme. But we couldn't say no, could we? Because generally – generally – it really did seem to cheer her up. And as the manager up at Deltey's wouldn't let her in the shop any more, she couldn't go and get it herself. She slipped us the money when she could instead, and let us know how she'd never manage without it: her medicine, her bit of comfort, the only comfort left. And did we mind, she'd ask, just running that one little errand for her, every now and again? Because the manager never seemed to mind us – it was just drunken people in his shop that he minded, not the ins and outs of selling the stuff. Besides, she said, she'd catch something called the DTs if she didn't have it, and they were so dangerous she might even die. And what could you say, to that? No?

'How's your old man today, then?' Aunty Net asked, breaking the silence that had fallen as she took her first couple of glugs and waited for them to settle.

Neither of us answered. James's eyes

strayed tellingly towards the television, over in the corner of the living room. It was on, but the volume was turned low. On the screen Rolf Harris tapered a virgin sheet of paper to his easel. A few swift, black scrawls, and Tweetie Pie emerged.

Aunty Net didn't take the hint. The drink had loosened her tongue and, once she was on the subject, she could rarely let the opportunity of badmouthing her brother-in-law go by.

'When's he back on nights?'

'He's on nights now, just working overtime today.'

'Bloody good thing too. Keep him out the way.'

James shrugged, his blond, cherubic features twisted into the sulky impatience typical of an eleven-year-old boy. At least, he was doing it because he thought it was typical. I knew because ever since his birthday he'd been adopting new mannerisms, different pouts and scowls, and an exaggerated slouch, making sure he looked his age and telling me I had to do what he said because he was so much older and wiser than me, now that he was eleven and – after the summer – entering Wesley Green Middle School.

He slumped into the back of the sofa and continued to stare at the telly, where Rolf Harris had finished his sketch and the cartoon had started.

Aunty Net sniffed disapprovingly.

'North wind blows and you'll be stuck with that face,' she muttered, fishing out a glass which was peeping from under the sofa, and pouring a second drink. 'Go on then, turn the sound up.'

After taking a hearty sip, she tried to engage us, one last time.

'You don't have to pretend. I know what he's like.'

Poor Aunty Net. Like a leftover from a Greek legend she spoke her truth and nobody believed her.

Ignoring her, we settled back to watch the rest of the afternoon's cartoons.

To the uninitiated, Blackbird Leys must seem like a prosaic place. A dismal, easily read, statistician's dream: a working-class suburb accessible to the rest of Oxford by a single bridge, one that, either side, was hardly ever crossed. The only place outside the estate that you could walk to, without crossing it, was The Works, the Austin Rover factory where everyone who wasn't on the dole ended up. Everything else people needed was there: three schools, primary, middle and upper, a church for weddings and funerals, a doctor's surgery, the Blackbird and the Bluenose Morris and, just before the bridge, a scraggly row of shops. There was Nash's Bakers, where everyone went for their Saturday treat, buying a big creamy éclair or a pink and yellow slice of Battenberg cake, and China House, for those special occasions when they could afford a takeaway. Or there was the chippy, for when they couldn't, but had a bit of loose change in their pocket that they didn't feel like blowing on the horses or a pint. There was the pharmacy, the newsagent-cum-Post Office, Deltey's and a Ladbroke's betting shop, next to the hairdresser's, which was run by Jimmy, known universally as Jimmy the Clip, a wispy-haired, slight man, who wielded clippers like they were weapons and could offer, for haircuts and styles, a choice of three: a crewcut, a basin and a shaggy dog perm for the ladies. You could ask for what you wanted, but those were what you got. Everything was there. There was no reason to cross the bridge, and more often than not, no money to catch the bus if you'd wanted to, anyway.

In amongst all this, teenage mothers wheeled their screaming babies up and down, prematurely crumpled faces perched gossiping on garden walls, their mouths spewing tidal waves of melancholy. An Income Support queue streamed out of the Post Office every Monday, a long river of dull-faced men, dribbling toddlers and aching women. Neighbours fought, bricks came through windows, houses were burgled, angry patches of graffiti decorated the shops and walls. 'Fuck off Pakis, go home', 'Tanya Ashworth is a dirty slag'. Couples let it all out on the streets, in the open air, screaming and shouting as they grabbed at each other's clothes. Arguments, normally, about who was going to feed the baby, who was going to pay the rent. Other times they'd be found reconciled, grinding frantically, pushed up against the walls of dark, narrow alleyways. 'Don't look,' Mum would whisper, cuffing the back of my head and dragging me on. Old, senile men, unrestrained, would undo their flies and take a leak on any corner, leave their pungent urine to curl down into paving cracks.

But there were other rhythms, as well, in our week. Things that only James and I knew about. We knew the secrets of the place, things statisticians could never guess at. We knew, for instance, the hidden weapon of the old Chinese grandfather at China House. We knew that the walking stick he leaned on was not really a walking stick at all. We knew that, at the slightest whisper of trouble, his geriatric limp would vanish and with a push of the button positioned at its oaken top, his stick would miraculously transform into a sword with which he'd chase off drunken vandals. He'd fly through the air, that old man, in a powerful display of arcanely acquired kung-fu skills. He'd pirouette around the floor, spinning over chequered tiles until his sword came to rest just a millimetre away from the offender's throat. He terrified everyone, James told me. He'd seen it all with his own eyes.

I knew other things, too. I knew that the three rotting tree trunks in my school playground were the homes of fairies, who slept through the day and flew out at night, up into the starry sky. I knew that the grassy mound next to the trunks, the pimple of a hill that we liked to roll down at breaktime, was really a sleeping giant's stomach, and that one day the giant would wake up and, rising and stretching his arms to heaven, shake off all the mud and flowers. And I knew, especially, all about the gypsies. If you walked around the back of our house you'd find another road, Hazelnut Path. Where normal people saw houses, I saw magical gypsy caravans, a parallel universe spilling out its rainbow of dangerous, brighter colours. There, one-eyed, gold-hooped women read palms, dark fiddlers strung their bows and spun out sinister lyrical mysteries. I could hear them, at night, at home in the dark, when I was supposed to be sleeping.

Pack of lies, Dick Roberts shouted when he heard me telling Mum, giving me a clip round the ear for my troubles. But at Aunty Net's everything was relative. Because of the mess and the corners stuffed with age-old treasures her house seemed infinite, magical, sprawling and twisting in defiance of convention, spreading out for miles. Aunty Net, like us, knew other things too, and though she only sometimes listened, she always put up with our rambling chatter.

2

The meal was silent. Dick Roberts sat, a blurred figure on the edge of my vision, slowly chewing through his food. Each rotation dared us to emit a sound. I could feel every thread of his salt and pepper hair; I could trace the etched lines of his diaphanous skin as they stretched across the bones of his face. His eyes were on us even though they were facing down. Eyes in the back of his head, he told us, and I knew he was telling the truth. Mum too, sat quiet and deadened in her chair, pushing gravied chips around her plate, tucking imaginary wisps behind her ears. We were all mute, captured and spellbound in his magician's circle, not daring to speak. I felt the slice of my knife so sharply it could have been cutting into my own skin.

James coughed, choking on some food. Dick Roberts's head jerked up, bowed down.

Sitting there, I wondered whether my parents had ever been in love, young and happy. It seemed impossible. I tried hard, and imagined them as rebels, like something out of *Westside Story,* rushing around Oxford slums in gleeful mockery, upturning cars and terrorizing neighbourhoods. In a time before his anger had a family to focus on.

Dick Roberts, his auburn hair dark with oil, slicked into an Elvis quiff: wearing a black, Teddy Boy jacket, he leans casually against a wall, looking over his dark shades towards Mum, sucking in his cigarette in a hazy cool cat motion. Mum totters coquettishly past, ponytail swinging, girlfriends on either arm. Briefly turning, she flutters false eyelashes at him while furiously chewing gum, looking suspiciously like one of the Pink Ladies in her bright ruffled skirt and toeless stilettos. Beneath her make-up her skin is young and flawless, her eyes sharp and pixie green.

I could feel her eyelashes as they fluttered. They flapped over my cheeks like butterflies, kissing my skin each time I finished a mouthful of food. It became a race against time, and I ate more and more quickly, with smaller and smaller mouthfuls, so as to maximize my kisses before the reverie was broken.

I could hear her tottering heels and

laughter echoing through the layers of time. Lost and homeless in our world, the sound vibrated helplessly around the room and died away.

Swallowing too swiftly, I hiccuped.

Dick Roberts's forehead creased and his eyebrows clenched together into a tight fist. A hand slapped down onto my cheek, a red flash stained my skin. Around me the room held its breath, all bar the tick-tick-tocking of the kitchen clock.

Tuesdays were speechless, silent and claustrophobic, like a brewing storm of pent-up accusations waiting to thunder down.

3

'I hate him,' James half whispered, half shouted. 'I hate him.'

'Shh,' I chided, as I folded a damp flannel and tried to dab at his burns.

One, two, three, four, five of them, plotted over his thin, luminously pale back.

He flinched away at the first touch and, scrambling across the bed, pressed himself into the darkness of the corner.

A full moon stared in through the window, a knucklebone face weaving shadows around the room.

I don't know what it is about cigarette burns, whether it's the look or the feel of them. They seem worse than any other injury, indelible, unlike the pouring blood of a deep cut even, which will at least vanish away with the wipe of a lovingly applied cloth. Cigarette burns didn't go away. They stayed there, large welts, sticky lesions weeping apricot pus onto areas of the body that remained invisible to everyone but us.

'I hate him, I hate him!'

'Shh! He'll hear us.'

He always did it on the back. He was clever, Dick. When he used his cigarettes he went for areas camouflaged by clothes.

'Here, you take it.' I leaned over, holding the flannel out to James.

'Leave me alone.'

'Please? I sneaked to the bathroom to get it for you. I could have got caught.'

'Go away.'

His voice was muffled. He'd brought his knees up to his chest and put his head in his hands, so that I couldn't see his face.

They were my fault, his lesions, and at the thought of them a guilty lump clogged my throat. Dick Roberts had arrived home early from doing his overtime and we'd been too busy playing to hear the click of the latch. James was my unwilling bride. I had dressed him in Mum's sequinned, early seventies wedding dress and was busy applying ruby lipstick to his cheeks in front of her vanity mirror. His platinum hair was trapped in pink plastic rollers, curling like Marilyn Monroe's.

Mum's bedroom was my favourite room. It was full of pastel colours and smelled of Yardley's talc and sugary girliness. It was her world, not his, a homage to the Pink Lady days when she was young and free. The bed was covered with fake peach satin and strewn with teddy bears and lacy pillows embroidered with affectionate tokens: 'I love you, Mum', 'To my darling daughter, on her birthday'. Catalogue clothes filled up the white, gold-trimmed wardrobe and there was a dressing table in the same style. It was littered with Avon lotions and cotton wool, and a tutued ballerina danced when you lifted the lid of the jewellery box. Elvis memorabilia plastered the walls, a framed jigsaw, a signed fan club poster. She even had a bedside alarm in his image, a flared, battery operated figure that gyrated whenever the alarm went off. It had been the worst day of Mum's life when he'd died. I was sitting on her lap, she told me, when Aunty Net rushed in, kicking up a song and dance about turning the news on. But when Mum had switched the television on and saw what all the fuss was about – she said she'd nearly passed out from the shock of it. A funny look came to her eyes when she talked about him, even now. Her first love, she called him, and I supposed that was why Elvis was James's middle name.

'This is such a girl game!'

'Shut up.'

It was as I was scolding James, pinching his arms to stop him ripping the rollers out of his hair, that Mum's head appeared, unannounced, from behind the door.

'That's my best lipstick!'

I let the lipstick slide from my grip and sheepishly countered, 'It was James's idea, it wasn't me.'

It was then that Dick Roberts pushed past Mum, and I realized with a plummeting heart that he was already home.

I could still see Dick Roberts's face, contorted with anger, as he thumped James onto the carpet and dragged him downstairs: his knuckles white as they gripped his hair his strength out of sync with his tall, bony physique. The wedding dress rose higher and higher, up over James's corduroys, with each jump. Frail sequins detached themselves and sprinkled, like confetti, over the floor. Standing on the landing top, I had watched and felt the stair ledges as they bumped over his body. There was a horrible pain in my throat. Mum stood next to me, wringing her hands helplessly, uttering impotent, wordless cries.

'They don't hurt too much now, do they?' I asked, but he didn't look up.

I waited for a moment more. When he still didn't answer I gave up and moved away, clambering up onto the top bunk as I tried to wash away the stamping motion of the cigarette. Dick Roberts, shouting about disobedience, deceit, slyness and ingratitude. About how we were thieving, lying little bastards.

These were our sins, and they had been tattooed into the quick of James's back.

We knew to steer clear of the cigarettes from past experience, but some days we were out of luck. And it was on Wednesdays, in particular, that we had to take special care. He was tired on Wednesdays. Anger steamed off him like a hot sweat, mingling with that special odour he had, a metal-and-grease, car factory edge. It was being up The Works that did it, Mum said, but it meant little to us. It was just the place where most of our dads went, the jagged line of square buildings and taupe chimneys on the edge of the estate, lurking at the peripheries of our life, belching shiny new cars onto the roads and charcoal smoke into blue days. However hard I tried, I could never quite imagine what went on inside the giant chimneys or behind the warehouse doors, what it was that made him so tired and mad. I had a vague impression of noisy, enormous machinery, crashing up and down, but that was all. All it meant to me was what I knew already, from being at home: splattered navy overalls; the packed lunches and flasks of tea Mum made for him each day; having to stay quiet because he was due on the nightshift and fast asleep in bed; those things, and the angry exhaustion that flickered into Wednesday's flame. I hated the factory for that final reason – what it turned Wednesdays into: the day when the beginning of the week seemed too far behind and the end too far ahead, when Dick Roberts's temper almost always snapped.

James rustled beneath me, moving back across the bed to crawl under his bedclothes.

Fighting broke out downstairs. Thumping and shouting echoed from the kitchen, intermitted by the low, persistent rattle of Mum's cough.

'I work all fucking day for this?'

'Don't, Dick, stop it, you're hurting me.'

I tried to think of other things, to shut it out and translate the grey, willowy shadows of our colourless room: my giant, silhou-etted, rose up from his sleep and scattered mud and rose petals over the playground grasses; the China House grandfather prowled noiselessly through moon-drenched streets; the midnight fairies sprinkled stardust through the starry night. In the distance, for just an instant, I heard the faint serenade of gypsies' violins.

James rolled over. I could tell from his breathing that he was crying.

'Read us a story, Jan.'

'I can't, can I? If he catches us with the light on—'

'Tell us one, then. Anything. One of Nan's ghost stories. Anything. It doesn't matter what.'

4

I shuffled in bed, folding my pillow in two, propping my elbow on it and my chin on my hand, looking into the darkness for inspiration. It didn't take long, there were only one or two ghost stories in our family, old timers, recounted after a drink or two at Christmas, along with other family anecdotes.

'What about the one in that village, where Nan was born?'

'The one about the bride?'

'Yeah.'

'That's good.'

'OK,' I said and, taking a deep breath, began.

I started in just the same way Nan B liked to, using the same tone of voice and words, which she'd honed through years of practice: 'It's an old village, right out on the outskirts of Oxford. And, in its centre, there's a very old church–'

'Which was cursed.'

'Shh.'

I tried to remember it as she told it. That

there was a story about the church. That it had once been a convent and that, way back then, a pretty young nun had been strangled by jealous friends.

'The body.' James wriggled beneath me, his tone brightening. 'Don't forget they bribed the builders and buried her in that new thing they were building. That vestry.'

'I'm supposed to be telling it, not you.'

'So?'

'I'll stop if you keep interrupting me.'

'Oh, shut up. Say what happens next.'

And so I did. I told him about how, after the nun disappeared, strange rumours started to go round the village. How some people said that they heard awful screams on certain nights of the year, and others talked of a shadowy female, walking in and out of the gravestones, clutching at her throat. How some novices went mad and were carted off to the mad house, where they soon passed way. How nobody listened to their cries about an avenging ghost; and when they died the eerie screams also died away, the ghostly figure was no longer seen, and all the rumours were eclipsed by the usual peace of the village, Minster Lovell.

'Fifty years went by, a hundred,' I continued, in what I hoped was a spooky whisper, 'until one day the daughter of the manor, a beautiful girl, got married.'

I could picture her as I said it, in my mind's eye: the delicate finery of her bridal gown sweeping over her slight figure, slender white silk, dazzling lace strewn with tiny pearls and glittering diamonds, all of it accentuating her natural grace.

'*Dick!*'

Mum's shout shot through the air.

There was a loud bang from the kitchen, followed by a clattering cascade, and then silence. We lay still, listening through the quiet. After a few seconds the front door slammed open and shut, fast footsteps sounded up the garden path under our window and disappeared around the corner, into the night.

'Do you think we should go and check?'

'No. She'll only tell us off for being out of bed.'

'S'pose.'

I pulled the covers up around my face. Outside, somewhere in the distance, a siren began to wail.

'Go on,' James prompted.

'I've forgotten where we got to.'

'The game they played – hide-and-seek.'

It was an old village tradition to play hide-

and-seek, as a part of any wedding festivities. Of course, the wedding couple didn't want to be disobliging. After letting their food go down the guests blindfolded the groom who, entering into the spirit of the thing, started to count to one hundred.

Everyone ran. It was only the bride who hesitated. Where could she hide? Where would her new husband never think of finding her? Biting down on her lips, she swept up her gown in one hand, lifting the twinkling diamonds from the floor and ran towards the vestry.

'Seventy-two, seventy-three, seventy-four...'

She could hear him counting, nearly a hundred now, but she still couldn't see anywhere.

She'd reached the vestry by then.

She stood there, out of breath, wiping the sweat from her forehead.

Then, suddenly, just as she was about to give up, she saw it.

Hidden away in a dusty corner was a plain-looking wooden trunk. It was small, but then so was she. Giggling to herself, she ran across the room, lifted the lid, and stepped in. It was just big enough. Lying down, she wrapped her dress around her legs, tucked her knees up to her belly, and closed the roof, over her head.

Nobody at that wedding ever saw her again.

The groom was heartbroken. For the rest of that day, and for weeks and months after, he wandered around the village calling out her name. He looked everywhere. He hired detectives to find her, and, when they couldn't, to try to uncover whoever had killed her. No one ever thought to look in the trunk, tucked away in the far corner of the vestry.

Not until fifty years later, that is.

'When one day, an old chest caught the new vicar's eye.' I was in the swing of it by then, remembering Nan's phrases and adding storybook words of my own. 'Striding over the stone floor, the vicar bent down and opened the locks, expecting to find some hymn books or something like that. But when he lifted the lid of the old wooden chest his eyes locked with the hollow globes of the–'

'Bride of Minster Lovell!'

I let out a scream as James lurched over the top of the bunkbed, covered in his bed sheet. It was pale blue, but in the dark it glowed luminous and white.

He bounced onto the mattress and on top of me, his knees digging into my ribs as he screeched like a banshee and pressed his pillow down onto my face.

'Get off, I can't breathe!' I struggled as hard as I could, but he was too strong.

I wrestled an arm free and grabbed onto him, pinching his thigh.

'Get off, or I'll shout for Mum!'

We at last rolled apart and sat, close together, our panting loud in the dark, waiting for Mum's voice to sound up the stairs, telling us off for making such a racket, but nothing came.

I could feel his hot breath on my cheek. My ribs hurt from where he'd sat on me and he'd ruined the end of my story, but I couldn't be angry. At least he wasn't thinking about his burns any more.

'Tops tails?' I managed to get out, at last.

'No. I'm too old.'

'Go on, just for tonight. I'm scared now.'

Half an hour later we lay, quiet and almost still. Dick Roberts hadn't returned and Mum's footsteps plodded slowly, wearily, upstairs to her bed. She clicked off the landing light, and the bright shaft of yellow disappeared from under the door, taking with it the few remaining evening shadows.

41

Our room was left properly dark, the night properly night.

I lay with my head twisted to one side, at an odd angle, so that James couldn't press his feet in my face. I could feel, through my growing drowsiness, the ligaments in my neck straining, aching ever so slightly.

'Night,' I whispered.

James's voice trailed back to me, soft and sure.

'Night.'

5

Mum had a strange dream the night before the Killings began. 'It was like the Pied Piper of Hamelin, only backwards,' she later announced, going on to describe a chaotic, crowded night vision, echoing with eerie music and dozens of screaming children as they ran away from, rather than towards, a strange piping man. She tried to look at him but his face kept twisting away from her, his features dissolving each time she verged on recognition. Flailing arms and stampeding feet fled across her mind and he disappeared into the hazy scarlet mist of frantic, fearful activity.

'I know you!' she shouted after his retreating figure.

She awoke with a start at four in the morning, glistening with sweat and crackling with an unclear foreboding. Pulling on her dressing gown, she rested her fingers against the thumping pain in her head, before tiptoeing down to the kitchen to make herself a cup of hot, sugary tea. There, balanced against the kitchen counter, she gulped back air and tried to steady herself as she waited for the kettle to boil. Sighing heavily, she leaned over the sink, and pulled up the window blind.

Outside the night was still and calm.

After an hour of watching, soothed by the tea and the silence, Mum slipped back up to bed, plugged her ears to block Dick Roberts's savage snores, and fell back into a deep, noiseless sleep.

'What have you done with them?' Aunty Net screamed.

She was standing at the gate of her house, lassoing her bulging handbag so that it spun around and around, above her head.

Then: wham!

Dick Roberts didn't duck in time. She hit him right in the centre of his forehead and he clutched at his skull, keeling over.

We watched them, transfixed, from our wooden ledge in the Hornet Swatting Tree.

'She must be drunk,' James murmured.

'But it's only morning.'

'Look at her. She must be.'

Aunty Net flung her handbag aside and crouched down, curling her tiny fingers around Dick Roberts's neck.

'I'll kill you!'

'Get off me, you crazy bitch!' Dick Roberts shouted, pushing her away.

She staggered backwards and, falling onto the pavement, let rip with a long stream of curses.

'You fucking bastard! You mean old cunt, picking on defenceless kiddies–'

They were making such a racket that a few people had turned away from the fence to watch them, and it has to be said that they were quite a sight. They seemed larger than life somehow, not out of character but almost double it, as though they had dressed up as themselves for a fancy dress party and were enacting a special scene for the occasion.

'She's mental,' James said. 'We're done for

now. It might as well have been us.'

'James! Janny!'

Beneath the tree Mum rushed about, wringing her hands as she shouted out our names.

'We should go down.'

'But he'll kill us if he sees us.'

I don't know what we would have done if it hadn't been that Nan B, at that instant, caught wind of the palaver and broke away from the crowd outside the park fence. She marched towards Aunty Net and Dick Roberts, her arms folded over her mint-green dressing gown, a neat row of pink rollers bobbing in the fringe of her hair.

'*Annette*. Get a hold of yourself. Look at the state of you, for crying out loud.'

She reached the other side of the road, and wrenched Aunty Net from the ground.

'But the kids are missing,' Aunty Net tried to explain. She started to brush at her skirt and shot Dick Roberts an evil glance, as Nan turned to scold Mum. ('*Katherine,* stop that bloody racket right now!') 'The kids have gone, Mum. Did you hear me? They weren't in bed when Katie went to check on them.'

Nan only stood, shaking her head and tapping her slippered foot.

'Well, what do you expect? They're probably out here with the rest of us, seeing what all the fuss is about.'

'But–'

'What were you thinking? That he'd gone and bloody murdered them?'

'I wouldn't put it past him.'

'I'll kill them when I get hold of them,' Dick Roberts muttered, rubbing the rising lump on his temple.

'See?'

But Nan had already turned, and was pointing a sharp finger towards him.

'You,' she said, 'can have a little more respect for the dead. I don't want to hear another peep from you – I'm not in the mood, Dick, and I'm warning you: if I hear that you've laid a finger on those kids after what's just happened, you'll be the second corpse in the mortuary today.'

Silence.

Dick Roberts and Nan B stared intently at each other, before he swerved his eyes away and, swearing under his breath, staggered back towards our house.

The scene beneath us was curious.

There was a park across the road from ours. It was a dirty oval of football pitches,

800 metres in perimeter. I knew it was that size, because the upper school, Peers, did their runs around it. It wasn't a bad park – there were two playgrounds in it, one up at the end of Cumberland Road, to the right of our house, beside the large blocks of dilapidated, leaking flats and opposite my school, Cumberland First School, and one right over the other side, on Cuddeston Way – but it looked quite barren and shabby, nonetheless. The railings flanking it were peeling, the white paint flaking off to reveal sickly under-colours of rust and black metal. They formed an inept barrier around the park, half falling, half straight, wavering and tottering like a drunkard going round and round in circles, trying to find his way home. The council hadn't planted any flowers, shrubs or trees, and the only greenery aside from the tattered, football-grazed grasses was the small, leafy brook that trickled through half of it and sliced one side of the fields neatly in two, like the first incision on a sponge cake.

This brook ended its life in a muddy, nettle-fringed pond opposite Aunty Net's. It was this pond that was arousing all the curiosity, because it had been cordoned off with yellow police tape.

Crowds of people pressed up against the railings. There were lots of them, fifty or more, young and old, most of them still dressed in pyjamas as they craned their necks and looked towards the ditch in portentous, collective intensity. Everyone we knew was there. Nan B was, and Aunty Net, along with other neighbours that we called Uncle and Aunty, and other people that we didn't know. They huddled together their arguments and fights forgotten as they dispatched incredulous whispers and sniffed the wind, for a tale behind the clamour.

'Naked...'

'Strangled, I heard one of them say.'

'They will go out at night, won't they, gallivanting off to God knows where–'

'–with God knows who.'

'Only fourteen.'

'The poor mother.'

And this was the thing, because the mother was Amber Jenkins's mother. Amber Jenkins, who had sometimes in the past sat with me on our garden wall, helping to brush my Barbie doll's hair, or plaiting my own strawberry blonde curls. Amber Jenkins, who was older and had long, straight hair, which was lovely and thick and very, very black. Who would tell me things that I didn't know, right up until she'd decided that I was too young for her and she too old for me.

Amber Jenkins's mother was the only person, aside from the uniformed policemen, inside the perimeters of the fence. She vacillated between clutching her stomach, leaning forward and loudly groaning, and making a run towards the white covered stretcher that lay on the ground beside the ditch. Each time she did this a policewoman caught hold of her, and she would let out a loud scream before crumpling into the restraining arms.

'My baby!' she cried, at intervals.

And other things, too: My daughter. My little girl. Oh God, please no.

Nan, having sorted Dick Roberts and Aunty Net out, had gone back to watching with the rest of the crowd. I watched as she said a few things to the person on her right, shaking her head at something before she looked back over her shoulder, I suppose to check on Aunty Net's whereabouts. As she did, her eyes flicked over the Hornet Swatting Tree. I thought she hadn't seen us but then she stopped, and her eyes shot back to where we were sitting. After glancing around quickly to check that Mum wasn't looking, she beckoned us down with a sharp wave of her hand.

'You've given your poor mother a hernia, looking for you,' she whispered harshly, when we joined her.

'Sorry.'

'You try telling her that.'

But she didn't call Mum over and, hidden amongst adult legs, we were able to watch as the still, blanket-covered mass on the dew-wet grass vanished and reappeared with the movement of people. It was so still and solid, the only substantial thing amidst the fluid business and purpose of the moving world around it. Amber Jenkins, from Hazelnut Path. I could almost feel the fibres of the cloth covering her, soaking up the moisture of the morning air and the beads of ditch-dirt from her dead skin. It seemed strange to me that I could feel the cold dampness, while she no longer could.

Behind us, Mum pushed through the crowd.

'Where have you been?'

'They've been here, you daft cow, under your nose the whole time.'

'Why didn't I see them, then?'

'Because you're as blind as a bloody bat,' Nan snapped, keeping her arms protectively around our shoulders. 'Leave the poor buggers alone. They'll get enough grief from their father without you chipping in as well.'

'They frightened me half to death.'

'You're frightening me half to death, flitting round in that bloody nightie. You'll catch your death of cold.'

The argument was cut short as around us, the crowd began to part and Mrs Jenkins was led home. Her eyes were red, and wild with distress. Her whole body was shaking with shock and her breaths came out in short, bewildered starts. She folded her shivering arms tightly around her middle, as though trying to protect herself from an invisible blow.

'If you could all go home now,' the policemen escorting her called at us, waving the hum of complaint aside. 'Have a bit of respect, will you? This isn't a circus.'

The stretcher had been lifted from the rainy ground, and two paramedics were carrying it towards a waiting ambulance. The silent blue sirens of police cars flashed over the road.

In drabs, we turned away from the scene and crossed the road to our homes.

6

Thursdays usually brimmed with an odd, emotional type of brutality. They were loaded with guilt, heavy with the violence of the preceding evening. Dick Roberts didn't usually hit us on Thursdays, but he watched us like a hawk. His hot glare snatched at and probed our every move, and each drop spilled from a cup, soap-sud drifting down from the sink, word spoken without first being spoken to, were used to justify his rage.

'I have to be cruel to be kind,' he'd say.

I was never sure who he was telling – himself, or us.

The Thursday of the Killings was out of the ordinary in every way. It wasn't just Amber Jenkins. There were other things. Dick Roberts didn't go back to bed, even though he was on nights. Mum didn't spend her day cleaning – the way she normally did – washing up or washing clothes or dusting and hoovering; making up new, superfluous tasks, like bleaching the crockery or reordering the kitchen drawers, when everything else was finished. James and I were allowed in the living room, which we never usually were. And Dick Roberts didn't raise his voice to us. Not once.

In fact, he wasn't like Dick Roberts at all. The only time when he looked himself, with that air of barely suppressed thunder, was when Mum had tried to make a joke and asked him whether he was feeling off colour. His lips had tightened then, and a brief tension pierced the air.

But it passed quickly, and despite our disappearance and the fight with Aunty Net, he didn't say a word against us. He called us into the living room after we'd eaten our Rice Krispies and pulled us down onto his armchair, planting an awkward, chapped kiss on each of our cheeks.

That was in the morning. The afternoon came and his mood still didn't change. He had Mum bring in our lunch – a ham sandwich, a mint Yo-yo and a packet of salt and vinegar crisps, the bread of the sandwich smeared thickly with margarine and cut into neat white triangles, just the way I liked it – and after we'd finished he pulled us back up on the sofa.

And there we stayed, one on each side, sitting stiffly with our hands in our laps.

Mum sat across the room, in the comfy armchair, watching *Sons and Daughters* on the telly.

It was a perfect August day. The afternoon sun filtered through the net curtains, lighting up the gas fire and grate and catching the silver bands of the fireguard so that occasional bubbles of light shot up, over the wallpaper and ceiling. The fire was off; it had been all summer. There were little wooden nooks on either side of it, which Mum had filled with neighbours' presents, keepsakes from different holiday destinations: a decorative plate saying 'Greetings from Margate'; a fairy standing on tiptoes in an open shell, 'Weymouth' spelled in red paint at her feet. We had a donkey somewhere, as well, though it wasn't in the fireplace. It was pink and the band on its straw hat read 'Viva España'. España meant Spain. That was the furthest place a present had ever come from.

The mantelpiece above the fire was cluttered with framed photos. There were lots of James and me, at age one, two, three, four, five, every single year of our lives, the later ones school photos. There was a black and white one of Nan B, standing in front of a line of drying sheets, squinting distrustfully at the lens with windswept, 1950s curls and lips that must have been heavily rouged, because in the photo they looked raven. Mum said the baby was Aunty Net, who was there in a frame of her own, beside the photo of Nan, a teenager in platform boots and a mini-dress. She was laughing wildly as she leaned forward to throw a white bouquet of flowers high into the air, and you could see the curve of her growing stomach against the tight fit of her dress. There was one of Uncle Terry, Mum's younger brother, and there were Mum's wedding photos and other ones too, of Nan B's mum and dad and her brother, Great-Uncle-Edgar-Who-Died-In-The-Second-World-War. Only Grampy B was missing. And the Roberts family, who were registered only by their absence, the blank slots of air where they had been, before Mum hid them away.

Mum rustled, shifting position.

She uncrossed her legs and recrossed them, the other way.

Her eyes flicked quickly, from the telly to where we were sitting.

I kept still, not wanting to disturb him any more than I had to. ('They looked like manikins,' I heard Mum say to Nan, later that night. 'You could have dressed them up and put them in a shop window. Stiff as a pair of corpses, poor little buggers. They didn't know what to make of it.')

I might have relaxed a little bit, but the thing was that Dick Roberts sat very still too. He always did. It was funny, the way he held himself. I had never seen him completely relaxed. There was always something on guard about him, something watchful in his expression – even when he was seemingly absorbed in the telly, or concentrating on something else.

His face was very freckled, like the rest of his body. Mum liked to say that if you joined them all up in a dot-to-dot, there wouldn't be any skin left. She said that his freckles were the exact same colour as his hair, before it had started to grey. (And if Aunty Net was there, she would usually respond, 'But is he a natural redhead, Katie? Can you tell us that?') Underneath the freckles his skin was pale, a half natural and half inflicted pallor, from council house nutrition and airless factory nights. He was thin, too. I could make out the bones of his thin, knuckly knees. They stuck out a mile from his trousers.

He must have felt me looking at him, because he stirred and lifted an arm to pat me clumsily on the head.

'All right?'

'Yes. Thank you.'

'Good,' he said, and went back to watching the telly.

I fingered the previous evening's bruise and wondered at the turn in events.

The doorbell rang and Mum got up to answer it.

It was Nan B; she followed Mum into the living room. I half expected her to register surprise, to say something like, 'What are you two doing in here?' when she saw where we were sitting, but she didn't bat an eyelid. She just stood, removing her headscarf, squinting out of the window at the sunny day as she patted her greyish white curls into place.

'What time you due up The Works, then?' she asked, by way of greeting to Dick.

'Seven,' Dick Roberts grunted, without looking up from the telly.

And that was it. They didn't say another word to each other. They hardly ever did.

Nan propped her folded trench coat over the sofa and sat down on the armchair Mum had vacated for her. She took off her glasses, and fished out a tissue from up her cardigan sleeve to give them a wipe.

'Well, well,' she muttered, shaking her

head and casting Mum a meaningful glance.

'I'd never have believed it,' Mum said.

'Well, you have to, don't you, Katie, in this day and age?'

'I suppose so.'

She started to say more, but Dick Roberts interrupted her, saying what about putting the kettle on.

Nan watched the telly while Mum was gone. It wasn't ever difficult to describe Nan, because she looked just like Mum. In fact Nan always said that if Mum wanted to know what she'd be looking like in twenty-five years she wouldn't ever need an expert, because it was staring her right in the face. They had the same petite build, the same short, curly hair, slightly pointed chin and long, patrician nose. Really it was only the hair colour and the crow's feet that were any different. That, and their bearing.

Sons and Daughters finished.

Dick Roberts got up to change the channels.

He flicked over them in turn, and decided on BBC2, where there was a snooker game in progress.

'I wonder how she is,' Mum pondered as she came back in, handing Nan and Dick steaming mugs of tea before perching back on the arm of the sofa.

Nan took a sip from her mug.

'Thanks, love,' she said, blowing on the steam. 'Just what I needed.'

'Have you heard anything?'

'I did better than heard.'

'What do you mean?'

'I went round there to see her.'

Mum started. It was hard to tell from her face whether she was shocked or impressed.

'You hardly know her,' was all she managed.

'The doctor was over there,' Nan continued, ignoring Mum's comment. She put her mug down on a coaster and settled back in her chair. 'And the next door neighbours. Doctor gave her a sedative. It's not going to last for ever though, is it? I'd hate to be there when that wears off.'

'What about the father?'

'They were asking her about that. It doesn't sound like she's even sure where he is nowadays.'

'I'm not surprised. He buggered off years ago,' Mum said. Then, unable to contain herself, she burst out, 'What was she playing at, though, letting her out till God knows what time of night?'

Nan shrugged. 'You can't blame her. They

all fly the nest at some point.'

'But still.'

'What can you do? Lock them in their bedrooms?'

'If that's what it takes.'

'You can't blame her,' Nan repeated.

Her word, as always, was final. They fell silent, focusing on the television.

'Anything good been on?'

'Nothing much.'

'Typical. They put bugger all on and still expect us to pay through our bloody noses.'

'Do you think it'll be on the news later?'

'What, Amber?'

'Yeah.'

'Think they'd put this place on the telly?'

'Yeah, but a murder–'

'Oh, Katherine.' Nan rolled her eyes. 'Don't make me laugh.'

Mum grunted. 'First time for everything.'

'Not bloody likely, my love.'

'The murderer,' James said.

We were lying in our beds, later that evening. Dick Roberts had gone to work. Intermittent voices floated up from the living room, where Mum and Nan still sat. 'I could get used to this, Katie,' I heard Nan say. They usually spent their evenings at the kitchen table.

'What about him?'

'He hasn't been caught yet.'

'No,' I muttered. 'So?'

'He might strike again.'

I rolled over, trying to get comfortable. I was tired and I didn't really want to talk. The day had worn me out and I felt funny, lying awake and thinking of Amber Jenkins on that ambulance stretcher.

Dead.

James, on the other hand, had the fidgets. He kept wriggling this way and that. Occasionally he slipped out of bed to look through the curtains, at the yellow tape and policemen standing on the other side of the road. They were collecting evidence, he said. I told him to get stuffed.

'He could kill anyone, next.'

'Shut up, will you? I'll shout for Mum if you keep waking me up.

'Cow.'

'Shut up.'

'He could kill *anyone*.'

'I don't care.'

But, in spite of myself, a sharp tingle rippled up my back.

'Do you get it?'

'No,' I said, even though I knew exactly

what he was getting at.

There was a pause, followed by a sharp rustle, and James's head reared up over the bunk.

'He could kill anyone, if you put it like that,' I said. 'Even you.'

'Not if we help him.'

'What are you talking about?'

'We could pray,' James said. 'To God, or something, and help him choose.'

'That's murder.'

I shut my eyes and rolled over, away from him, opening them when he couldn't see to stare at the wallpaper pattern, close to my face: tiny threads of peach blossom snaking upwards, the perfect symmetry breaking at the gluey joins in the sheets. I remembered Dick Roberts doing it, last year. How getting the flowers aligned had been fiddly, how he'd lost patience and blamed Mum for deliberately choosing that pattern.

'Don't pretend you don't know what I'm talking about.'

When I didn't answer he reached out and pinched the top of my arm.

'Stop it!'

'We'd be free, Jan. We'd never be frightened again.'

'We'd be murderers.'

'We won't have done anything wrong, not if it's God we're asking for the favour.'

'It would be wrong.'

'Don't be stupid. Anyway, we'd get to perform rituals and stuff like that.'

The thought of it.

He'd been kind to us, that afternoon.

'Just shut up, will you?' I snapped. 'I'm tired. I want to go to sleep.'

'But—'

'I'll shout for Mum. I swear to God I will.'

'Spoil sport,' James grumbled.

But he gave in, and climbed back down to his own bed.

I dreamed of Dick Roberts later that night. He was stroking my hair, and his hands were soft and light. But then he changed without any warning, lost his temper and slapped me hard in the face. I turned and ran away from him, out of our house and across the road to the ditch. Fighting my way through the tangle of sharp brambles and stinging nettles, I came to where Amber Jenkins was lying, floating in the soupy mud. Her eyes stared unblinking to heaven and her hair spun out around her in long, dark webs. A breeze nudged her ever so softly from side to side, her blue face haloed in the evening light.

7

Uncle Terry was Nan B's prodigal son. He toured the country as a drummer in a country band, playing at wedding and birthday celebrations. Occasionally he would pass through and appear at our door, spilling over with toffees and tales of pretty girls. The world was full of smiles on those days, and Aunty Net, Nan B and Mum would ply him with food and adoring love for the short time that he stayed. Aunty Net almost regained her sanity when he visited. She'd rest her arms on the sideboard and chat easily, her troubles temporarily forgotten. Uncle Terry smiled cheekily from his corner, tossed sweets in our direction and disappeared off again, somewhere into the map of England, after he'd eaten his meal.

During or after those visits there would always be nostalgic references to the good old days, and it was then that they talked over the old stories, like the Bride of Minster Lovell, or the Tale of the St Clements Ghost. The St Clements Ghost one would always come up, in fact, because of the role Uncle Terry played in it. It was usually Nan who told it.

She remembered it was a Friday, because it was Friday the thirteenth. She'd had a terrible sinking feeling all through that day and right into the night. She couldn't concentrate on anything. She burned the tea and almost set fire to the kitchen with the chip fat. Not looking where she was going, she tripped and nearly fell down the stairs. She couldn't put her finger on what was wrong, and eventually dosed off into a fretful sleep, on her armchair, in front of the Calor gas fire.

Uncle Terry, for his part, was elsewhere in Oxford on that day and night, preparing for combat.

He'd recently moved into a flat near the centre of Oxford, in St Clements. It was dark and dingy, with a strong, musty atmosphere, but it was also large and extremely cheap.

'Yes,' he said, clutching the agent's hand and shaking it rigorously. 'Yes, I'll take it.'

On the day that he moved in he noticed a puddle of dry, old blood at the bottom of the oak stairwell. He tried to contact the owner who, like most landlords, failed to return his calls.

'Never mind,' he thought, in the end. 'Probably easily explained. Someone had a nasty fall, that's all.'

Uncle Terry was never one for vigorous analysis. He shrugged his shoulders and turned to walk up the stairs. He soon forgot about the dark brown blood as he dissolved into the persuasive rhythm of his drums.

Of course, that wasn't the end of the matter.

It was only the very beginning.

'How do we begin?' I asked James.

We were sat on a patch of dirt behind the garden shed, hidden from sight of the living-room window. You'd have been able to see us from Nan's. She lived on the higher level of the double-stacked maisonettes behind our house, and her kitchen sink overlooked our back garden. It would have been a problem if she'd seen us, but we'd chosen a time when she'd come round and was in our kitchen, with Mum. So we knew we were safe from prying eyes, even though we conceded that somewhere else would have been better – somewhere more mysterious and secret.

'I don't know,' James hesitated, suddenly uncertain. 'I suppose – I suppose we could start with that thing they say in Church.'

'What's that?'

'You know, what's it called? The Lord's Prayer.'

We'd learned it at school.

It was my turn to hesitate and I stood there, looking at him. He was short for his age, fair and thin, and his arms and legs were covered with dark, ruby grazes – totems from Dick Roberts and our scuffles with each other. Last summer we had tried to collect all of our scabs together, picking and storing each one as they ripened. We wanted to make a voodoo necklace but somehow we never managed to get enough pieces. I was three years younger and almost as tall as he, but in spite of his diminutive figure he looked much older than most his age. It was his eyes. They'd gathered age and depth quickly. I wondered if mine were the same.

Standing there watching him, this thought occurred to me: I was saving him, and he was saving me.

We clasped our hands together, and began.

Uncle Terry's first day passed peaceably and when evening came he left the flat and walked down to his new local, the Half

Moon. He passed the night pleasantly enough, drinking Guinness and sharing stories with strangers. When he returned to his home it was quiet and dark. The streets were bare and the moon washed the hallway window with a stream of silver. Smiling contentedly to himself, he shut the door behind him, and went upstairs to bed.

At around four o'clock in the morning he was woken by a strange sound. There was someone else in the house. He could hear loud footsteps clanking up the stairs. Shivering beneath his covers, wondering what to do, he listened as the steps reached the landing and walked slowly into the second bedroom, beside his own. He sat up hurriedly in bed.

'Who's there?' he shouted.

'What next?' I asked.

James was surer of himself now, gaining in confidence.

'We have to do a dance,' he said, 'and chant, "Dick Roberts Must Die," over and over, twenty times.'

He grabbed my hands and we began to spin.

There was nobody there.

Bursting into the second bedroom with sudden resolution, Uncle Terry found nothing but a lonely space, a decrepit bed and an empty wardrobe. The only sound was the jagged catch of his breath and the frantic thumping of his rapidly pacing heart.

'Must have been dreaming,' he muttered to himself, rubbing his eyes.

The locals of the Half Moon had a different story to tell him the following night when they heard where he was living. That was no dream, they told him. That was the spirit of Ronnie McLewis, the St Clements ghost. Old Ronnie, a provincial villain, had been pushed down those stairs many years ago. Now his ghost wandered up and down them, every night.

Uncle Terry laughed nervously and shook his head.

'Bullshit,' he said.

He was sick of the silly ghost stories of his own bloody family without having to deal with any more. Downing his pint and wiping the froth from his mouth with the back of his hand, he resolved to go back to the flat and put an end to the mystery.

'The final bit,' James told me, his blue eyes fixing mine.

We leaned against the garden shed, catching our breaths. James rummaged through his pockets and his hand finally emerged holding a tissue-wrapped package. It contained threads of Dick Roberts's hair, stealthily retrieved from his pillow and comb.

'Final bit,' James repeated.

Uncle Terry did not sleep in his bed that night. He lay awake, instead, in the second bedroom. At four o'clock the footsteps returned, clanking their way up the stairs and into the room, towards his bed.

'Jesus f★ ★ ★ing Christ,' he thought, as they moved closer and closer. 'What am I supposed to do now?'

He struggled and screamed as the invisible figure lay down on the mattress and pressed onto him – or into him – and Uncle Terry found himself being lifted, by some strange force, into the stale air.

'Terry!' Nan cried, waking up from a nightmare and making towards the door.

Somehow Uncle Terry managed to escape. Tearing down the stairway, racing past the dark shadow of blood, he struggled with the front door handle and threw himself out into the street just as Nan B drew up in a taxi.

'Mum!' he choked, as she pulled him into the car.

They sped off into the night and never returned.

We watched as the tiny mound of hair and dry straw smouldered and blackened on the ground.

'That's it,' James said. 'We've done it, that's our offering. It's just a matter of time now.'

'What if nothing happens?' I asked.

'You wait,' James laughed. He leaped up and punched the air, his face a wide grin. 'He'll be next. I promise.'

I bit my lip and watched the last licks of smoke vanish.

'James, Janet!' Mum called from the doorway. 'What are you buggers up to, hiding behind the bloody shed? What's that smell?'

'Nothing, Mum!' James shouted.

He jumped forward and quickly kicked the straw pile apart, stamping the sooty remnants into the ground.

'Get in here, now.'

'Coming.'

James grasped my hand, giving it a squeeze.

'OK?' he whispered.

I nodded my head, and we turned and ran inside.

8

The park had been conquered, the scuffed grasses and last few traces of murder – scattered carnations, mournful cards – supplanted by a sunny clutter of stalls and rides. James and I watched all day from the kitchen window as caravans arrived, alongside massive lorries adorned with fantastic lettering. 'Guiseppe's World of Wondrous Waltzers' drove past our door, along with other foreign, exotic-sounding alliterations. Strange men with long hair and mottled blue tattoos hopped out from vehicles, skimming up and down the fairground rides with the agility of acrobats, shouting out instructions to each other with harsh, deep voices. Wild-looking, moss-coloured children skipped around the patches of grass that remained. They wore ragged clothes and screamed and laughed together, and were allowed to run wild while their parents concentrated on other things.

They looked magical to me, shouting and fighting like that, scrambling around in all their luxurious, unkempt glory. I secretly speculated that they were the friends of the gypsies, the invisible community that lived behind our house. I told myself that the gypsies would come out of hiding now that the fair people were here. I lay in bed at night, thinking about it, imagining how it would happen. By the end of the week I'd grown so excited that what was at first consciously make-believe became almost real, and I found myself standing sentinel at the window for half the day, so as not to miss out if they did actually appear.

'Some of us have got work to do,' Mum chided every now and then, shooing me out of the way so that she could get to the sink.

Since Amber Jenkins's death, Mum's own imagination had been working overtime. She'd caught a nasty chill from going outside in her nightdress that morning and Nan said she'd caught paranoia as well. She was referring to the fact that Mum was fretting more than ever. She had worked herself up into a lava about Amber, finally persuading herself that there was a Blackbird Leys serial killer on the loose and that the police, loath to visit the estate at the best of times, weren't doing anything about it. She grew so convinced that she used her illness as an excuse to keep us inside.

'I won't be able to see what they're up to,' she'd said to Nan, in between blowing her nose in a hanky and coughing up a new load of phlegm. 'Look at the state of me. I wouldn't have the energy to go chasing after them if they got into trouble, even if I wanted to.'

'It's their summer holiday,' Nan had defended us. 'And anyway, since when have you ever gone out chasing them?'

But it was no use and, aside from her one concession of letting us roam the back garden, we stayed in for almost two weeks. It wasn't until the third and final night of the fair that curiosity got the better of Mum.

Nan was partial to fairs herself. She came over every night of the week that it was there, taking my place at the window when she arrived, gazing out at the colours and the winking lights when she wasn't busy chiding Mum: for being a misery guts in general, and for not going up the doctor's and sorting out that damn cold. 'It's gone on long enough,' she complained. 'And anyway, it's driving me up the wall. Do you think I want to come over here and listen to you hacking away all day?' She would have stayed home, she said, and watched from her own kitchen window – and she'd have preferred it, for all the fun that Mum was, lately – if it weren't for the fact that our bloody house was blocking her view.

On Saturday, when Dick Roberts had gone off to do his overtime and twilight was setting in, she decided to have one more go.

'Surely it wouldn't hurt?' she asked, turning from the window to raise her eyebrows at Mum, who was sitting in her dressing gown at the kitchen table. 'Just for a little while?'

'Oh, Mum, give it a rest, will you?' Mum snapped, tiredly. 'You're worse than the kids.'

She sneezed, and went back to her cup of Lemsip. We'd looked up from our game of Connect Four to listen but, hearing Mum's response, carried on playing. We knew from past experience that there wasn't much point in trying to persuade her otherwise, once she had an idea in her head. It wasn't until she'd finished her drink and walked over to the kitchen window to have a look outside that our hopes began to rise.

Fairs didn't come our way all that often.

There was the big one up in town on St Giles every year, but that was it. We were lucky if we saw one in Blackbird Leys once a year, and when they came they were so colourful and spectacular, in comparison to anything else that ever went on, that it was hard not to be drawn to them.

'Look at that Ferris wheel,' Mum muttered, twitching the net curtain.

'Big, isn't it?'

'Look – there's Shirley over there. Knocking on a bit for the fair, isn't she?'

'Never too old for it.'

Mum snorted disparagingly, but she carried on watching all the same.

'God, they don't half make a racket, don't they?' she said, after a pause.

'It's the last night, as well. They're going to turn it right up.'

And, as if in response to Nan's words, the volume did suddenly shoot up. They always turned it up at dusk but she was right, and it did seem especially loud.

'Bloody hell,' Nan winced. She let the net curtain drop and moved away, glancing at Mum out of the corner of her eye as she flicked the kettle on. 'It's a shame that they chose now to go and set up shop here, isn't it? Any other time and we'd be out there having a bit of fun, instead of in here where we can't even hear ourselves think. Oh well, it can't be helped. Do you want a cup of tea? One more cup, and I suppose I better be off.'

Mum didn't answer.

She took a couple of steps away from the window but then stopped and turned around, to take another look.

'I'm not even dressed,' she said.

Nan wasn't ever one to look a gift horse in the mouth. Seeing Mum's hesitation, she dropped the mugs on the sideboard and had chivvied her out of the kitchen almost before we had chance to take it in.

'It won't take you ten minutes to get some clothes on,' we heard her say, as they disappeared upstairs.

'Bit of fresh air will do you good,' Nan shouted.

She had chattered on and on since we'd left the house, hardly pausing for breath, making sure that Mum didn't have a chance to get a word in edgeways or, most importantly, to change her mind about coming out.

We held on to their hands, like we promised we would, and wove our way in and out of the crowds.

It was packed. Practically everyone from

the estate must have been there, young and old. People clustered together and others walked here and there. They were busy eating, or queuing for rides, hopping from one foot to another as they struggled to stay comfortable in their bare legs and muddy stilettos, chatting to each other as they checked their change to see how much money they had left.

'God, you do get through it, don't you? I've spent most of my money already,' I heard one girl saying to another.

The strong, hot smell of frying fat came at me in heady wafts, taking the cool edge off the late summer breeze.

A myriad of sounds clambered for attention. Different soundtracks competed, conversations bounced against each other, frequent shouts sounded out as traders plied their rides and stalls, and their customers spotted familiar faces in the crowd.

'Look!' James giggled, as Mum and Nan stopped to say hello to one of our neighbours.

He pointed to a girl who was bending over the twister railing, retching. Her friend stood patiently beside her, wearing a pair of glittery deelyboppers – which sprung like strange antennae from her hair – chewing her way through a wad of fluffy pink candyfloss. The ride had just stopped and I supposed they were amongst those getting off.

A fairground hand saw her and bounded up the steps, taking her by the arm.

'Come on, out of it!' he said with a jovial shout. 'You're giving us bad publicity!'

My view was blocked before I could see what happened next, and we moved on.

There was so much to look at, so many rides: the waltzers screamed music and blurred with speed; grim, painted faces leered from the walls of the ghost train; the Ferris wheel sloped up and down through the heavens. There were stalls full of cuddly toys, and others full of dolls, and others full of goldfish, which swam to and fro in their tiny plastic bags. ('Poor things,' Mum said, but Nan replied that they only had fifteen-second memories, and that there were better things to worry about.) There were arcades full of fruit machines and computer games and other glass machines, where you put your pennies and twopence pieces through a slot at the top and watched to see whether they would dislodge the tiers of coins below – even though usually they only clattered down and came to a rest on the top pile. The arcades seemed to fizz and rattle with the noise and lights. Cash jangled, machines whirred and rainbows of light popped on and off in epileptic splendour, belying the deeper, electric hum that lay at the base of it – a loud, constant purr that I couldn't really hear until I listened for it.

'Let's get you two a toffee apple each,' Nan said, in a sudden fit of generosity. She stopped walking and shot us a brief smile. 'You've been in for two bloody weeks, summer holidays as well. You deserve a bit of a treat.'

She rifled through the contents of her handbag, the red strobe of the dodgem cars playing across her cheek. Mum stood beside her, trying to scowl and blow her nose at the same time.

'Spoilt rotten,' she grumbled.

Nan didn't hear her.

'Aren't you glad we came, Katie?' she said.

Mum was about to reply – and it looked like it was going to be in the negative – but, just as Nan pulled out her purse, Uncle Stan, next door but one, passed by.

'Have you heard?' he called.

He caught Mum's quizzical expression and added, over his shoulder, as he disappeared, 'They found another body, didn't they? Half hour ago.'

80

'What we going home for?' Nan panted, as she struggled to keep up with Mum. 'What do you think he's going to do, jump out from a fair ride and strangle the bloody lot of us?'

'Stop telling me what to do, will you?'

'What did Stan say? What's happened? Who is it?'

'They're not your kids, they're mine, and I'll bring them up how I like.'

'I can't keep up, you're going to give me a heart attack.'

'I can't help that.'

But she had to stop, because James ground to a sudden halt. He'd been quiet and un-complaining as Mum dragged us from the fair. I'd tried to catch his eye after Uncle Stan told us the news, but he wouldn't look at me. Now, his face crumpled, his cheeks reddened and he began to howl.

'Christ.' Nan watched him, aghast. 'Katie, what the–?'

But she wasn't going to get an answer from Mum. All of the running had caught up with her; she had doubled up in a vicious burst of coughing and was only able to mutely shake her head, as tears streamed down her face.

'I don't want to go home,' James screamed.

A jet of snot shot out of his nose. He was crying so hard that he began to choke.

It worked, I thought, as I watched him. It worked.

And I felt my first stab of real terror.

'Oh Jesus,' Nan said, as I let out a sob.

We've killed him, I thought.

We're murderers.

'You as well, you silly bugger?'

I opened my mouth to speak, but nothing came out.

'Our dad,' James spluttered, from where he'd fallen onto the grass.

'What?' Mum started, but she was overtaken by a new wave of coughing and had to turn away.

'What about your dad?' Nan asked. Her face clouded in puzzlement but then cleared, as realization began to dawn. By the time Mum had recovered she had worked out what was going on.

'They think it's their dad who's been killed,' she said with a contemptuous snort, as she grabbed James by his armpit and, pulling hard, finally succeeded in wrenching him up from the ground. 'Where the hell do they get it from? It's not my side of the family, I'll tell you that.'

9

Dick Roberts got into a temper the following afternoon.

It was our fault, really. It all started over the lighter we'd used to burn the threads of his hair. We should have put it back in its usual place afterwards, but James had wanted it as a special keepsake. There were plenty of lighters and matches in the house and Dick Roberts hadn't missed it at first. In fact, I had almost forgotten about it altogether when, on Sunday – when he was already in a bad mood – he noticed it was gone.

'Where have you put it?' he asked Mum, his voice riddled with impatience.

When she couldn't answer he got up from his chair and started to hunt for it, so as to make a point. At first he did it half-heartedly, huffing and puffing, casting his eyes here and there, but then, as his pique grew, so did his determination: he upturned the sofa cushions, pulled the photos off the mantelpiece and emptied the contents of the kitchen drawers, leaving cutlery and tea towels strewn over the kitchen floor, for Mum to tidy up later.

'It's got to be somewhere,' he kept saying.

He grew angrier and angrier, and then, finally, began to work his way upstairs,

It was then that James started to look apprehensive.

'Oh, for God's sake, Dick, it's not the end of the world,' Mum tried to dissuade him, as we followed him from room to room. 'Come on, love, I'm not well. It's Sunday – you need your rest. Let's go and sit down.'

But he ignored her. And eventually, after another half hour of searching, he found it. In its hiding place, slipped slyly beneath James's pillow.

And that was when all hell broke loose.

'I'll teach you about stealing!' Dick Roberts had lunged down the stairs after James, who had shot into the living room and was crouching pathetically behind the sofa, with his hands over his ears and his eyes shut tight.

He rushed past, grabbing my hand and bending the little finger as he shoved me to one side. It snapped as easily as if it were a frail matchstick, or a dry wishing bone. I was so scared that I hardly felt it until later.

'Stop it, Dick. For God's sake, please!' Mum shouted.

She ran into the living room after him and pulled at his arm, trying to coax him away. Dick Roberts whirled around at her touch. He brought up his fist and smashed it, hard against her lips. She flew backwards and crumpled against the back wall, sliding to the carpet, and was quiet.

It could have gone on for ever but at last the next door neighbours started banging on the adjoining wall. 'You nosy bastards,' Dick Roberts screamed, letting go of the neck of James's jumper and rushing to the mantelpiece, pummelling his fists against the wallpaper above it. But it worked. The interruption upset his momentum and, giving one final roar and kicking at the air with his boot, he stormed out, slamming the front door, fracturing the glass pane behind him.

'I told you to put it back,' I whispered, admonishing James later that day.

The house was eerily silent. The television was off, so there wasn't even that to break the quiet. Mum sent us up to our bedroom and was downstairs in the kitchen, licking her own wounds, alone.

'It was my memento,' James stammered back at me, still defiant. 'Needn't have nicked it, anyway,' he added.

We were on the top bunk, my bed. I sat, propped against the wall, while James lay beside me. He looked bad. His face was blurred with bruises, transformed and made strange with a series of swellings. Raven scabs protruded from his nose. Some of his blood had come off on my bedclothes, and left dark streaks over the quilt pattern.

'Shouldn't have bothered. It didn't work, did it?'

'No,' I paused. 'But it might, still.'

'Don't be dumb,' James snapped. 'It was just a game, something to do.'

'Keep your hair on.'

'I wish it had worked and that he was dead,' he said, before he buried his face back in the pillow.

I closed my eyes, trying hard to think of all the good things in our life. However hard I conjured they would not come. There was no giant scattering rose petals over the hill, no midnight fairies, no strange gypsies or crying violins. Even the ghost stories were hard to focus on. They were all just silly – nonsensical, fragile things – just words. Words, and nothing else.

'I'm going,' James's voice came, warm on my cheek.

I opened my eyes.

He was sitting up and watching me closely.

'I'm going to run away with the fair.'

'Don't be stupid,' I said.

'What's so stupid, stupid? Better than staying here.'

'You're only eleven.'

He shrugged. 'So?' he said. He smiled for the first time that afternoon. He had that look on his face, the one he got whenever he had a new idea, and I began to realize he wasn't just having me on. 'Don't tell Mum. Promise.'

'You might get kidnapped. By someone bad.'

'I can't imagine meeting anyone worse than my own dad.'

I couldn't think of an answer to that.

'How will you do it without Mum seeing you?'

He hesitated, thinking it over. 'I'll climb through the window and down the drainpipe. You go and call her when I'm near the bottom, and I'll run through the gate while she's gone.'

'Why should I?'

'Go on.'

'I'll get into trouble.'

'Go on. Please. You can say I left when you were asleep.'

'What am I going to do when you're gone?'

'You'll be all right.'

'No, I won't. It'll just be me and him.'

'Anyway, I'll come back and get you.'

'No, you won't.'

'Don't start crying, Janny, please? Do this for me. Just this once?'

I'd followed him down from the bed to the window, and stood to one side as he opened it. A breeze blew in from the gap. It was still warm, but I could feel the beginnings of a cool evening.

'You'll get cold,' I sniffed, but he didn't hear me.

He groaned like an old lady as he pulled himself out of the window and, feeling for a foothold, started to clamber slowly down the drainpipe. He winced with each move, but he was careful: the pipe rattled and clanged a little bit, but not so much. Even if Mum did hear it, it was quiet enough for her to think it was just a tomcat or something similar.

In the near distance, over in the field, fair-hands dismantled the last of the rides. They shouted to each other in the same way as they had when they were setting them up, hopping and climbing, running here and there, the late sun casting honeyed tints over their muscled torsos.

A couple of new bunches of carnations had been tied to the railings, brightening up the old bunches, which had started to brown.

A few boys played rounders at the end of our block. Engrossed, they didn't look our way.

James neared the bottom of the pipe. He looked up and smiled pleadingly.

'Please?' he mouthed.

I looked down at him.

After all, I thought, he'll probably only last for a couple of hours, a night at the very most.

'Please?'

He'd jumped down and was waiting by the front door, looking up at me with his hands pressed to his chin, prayer style.

I ran to the wardrobe, plucking a jumper from its hanger.

Just a night at the very most, I thought.

And then he'd be back, and he'd have had his fun and be grateful to me for not squealing.

I ran back and threw it down to him, hardly pausing to wave goodbye – I knew if I did I'd start crying properly – before I turned and walked through the bedroom door, out onto the landing.

'Mum!' I shouted.

'What?'

'Mum!'

'What is it? What do you want now?'

She appeared, after a moment, at the foot of the stairs.

'I,' I started. 'James ... James is picking on me.'

'Oh, for God's sake.'

'And my hand is hurting.'

It was. I suddenly noticed how much it was throbbing. 'Do you wonder that your father gets into these moods, do you? What with the way that you two carry on? Get back into bed.'

'It really does hurt. Honest.'

'I don't want to hear another peep out of you two, you hear me?'

'But–'

'You hear me?'

'Yes.'

'Now get back in bed.'

10

Mum stormed around the house, clutching her dressing gown with shivering hands as she ran up and down, down and up the stairs. She looked in the three bedrooms, the living room, the kitchen, the bathroom, the toilet and finally, unlocking the back door, launched herself up the patio and wrenched open the garden shed, peering anxiously inside.

Nothing.

Pulling open the front door, she stood at the rusting garden gate and twisted her head right and left, up and down the road.

She rushed back in again and embarked on a second check.

Nothing.

'Where is he?' She leaned over me, and with her hands on my shoulders, gave me a shake.

She clenched her face into a tight ball in an effort not to cry. The wrinkles spun over her face, like a dense spider web. Her breath started to jar and she dug her fingernails through the thin material of my nightdress. I thought she was either going to scream or hit me.

I reached up a hand to my sticky cheeks. The movement revived the pain in my finger.

'You would tell me, wouldn't you, if you knew?'

I nodded, rubbing one eyelid. She opened her eyes and looked hard at me. Her dark, contracted pupils flicked slowly over my new bruises before she straightened up and, running her fingers through her raven hair walked to the telephone.

'Who can blame the little sod?' she muttered, picking up the receiver and clumsily fumbling for the holes, dialling out a number.

7-6-3-8-8-1.

She stood, softly wheezing, picking at her nails.

One, two, three rings.

I moved from the stairs and sat down on the carpet near her feet, and traced the eddying whirlpools of blue with the hand that wasn't hurting. Ragged strands of pink dangled down from her threadbare dressing gown. Flakes of white skin peeled off her heels. They curled over themselves, like tiny wood shavings.

Four rings, five.

'Come on. Pick up.'

Six, seven.

Eight, nine, ten, and still no answer.

'Shit!' she cried, slamming the phone down.

Her body sagged as she struggled to stave off a new fit of coughing and tears.

'Come on,' she said, wiping her eyes and pulling me off the floor. 'We're going out. Let's get your coat on.'

Three cups of tea later. The only sound was the laboured rhythm of Mum's tear-laden breathing. Occasionally Nan B let out a loud sigh. Other than that it was quiet, so quiet it almost seemed as though life had been stopped in its tracks, and the two women floated rather than sat, the world around them breathless and heavy.

'Well, I don't know, where has that little bugger got to?' Nan eventually asked.

It was midnight. We were round at Nan's, sitting in her kitchen.

Nan's was funny. Not because it was anything out of the ordinary but because she seemed out of place in the block of maisonettes, a bit too prim for the stairs that you had to walk up to get to hers, sidestepping the puddles of spit and phlegm and the shards of broken bottle glass, a bit too proper for the fights and music you could always hear coming from the other homes, and the damp plywood that boarded up broken windows. She didn't like it but, as it was either that or live away from us up on the Barton estate in Headington, she made the best of a bad job while she waited for her council transfer to come through. The four little rooms were spotlessly clean. She'd decorated them with presents from the foreign language students she used to take in, before she decided she was getting too old: Japanese fans; fragile white duck eggs, mounted and painted with water-garden scenes; a couple of embroidered mountain landscapes. There were other things, too – a set of old-fashioned wedding china on display, school photos of us and Aunty Net's children, and snapshots of the rest of her family, apart from Grampy B, Dick Roberts and Aunty Net's two husbands, who weren't there (not even in the wedding photos, which were just of the brides, alone). A lot of the photos were black and white, and similar in style to the ones we had. But all that was mainly in her bedroom and the living room. The kitchen was quite bare, with monotone magnolia walls and an insipid beige sideboard. There was a bit of greenery above the overhead cupboards, a spider plant and a dangling ivy. A kitten calendar was pinned to the wall, with all our birthdays written out in blue biro, and there was the Swedish cuckoo clock one of her students had brought her, but that was all.

'Must be a lock-in at the Blackbird,' Nan commented. She glanced up at the clock as she came back in from trying our number one more time. 'You sure you've left a note where that little bugger can see it?'

Mum nodded.

'Best not to tell Dick tonight if you can help it, anyway,' she said. She scowled sourly at Mum's bruised features. 'He'll be in no fit state, if you're anything to go by.'

Mum grunted and tilted her face to a different angle, trying to hide the marks running down her left side. Her upper lip had swollen quite badly from where he'd punched her. There was a nasty, bloody scab in the top corner.

'He's run away, hasn't he?' Nan said, picking up her empty mug and peering into it.

She looked just like she did the morning

they found Amber Jenkins's body. She was wearing her mint-green dressing gown and furry slippers; the usual pink row of rollers was busy curling her hair. We'd woken her up, coming round. She'd opened the door with sleepy eyes (after clicking on the hallway light and calling, 'Who's that?' through the letterbox) and explained that she hadn't picked up the phone because she'd thought it was only Annette.

'Silly bugger's gone and run away.'

'Go on,' Mum said, her voice thick as she reached for a tissue from the pack Nan had brought down from her bedroom. She hadn't said much since we'd arrived. I wasn't sure whether it was because she was too upset, or just that it was difficult to speak. 'State the bloody obvious.'

'Don't you go getting at me, my girl. It's not my fault if your kiddie thinks he'll be better off on the streets.'

'You love rubbing my nose in it, don't you?'

They bickered on. I scrutinized my hand, biting back tears. It was hurting more and more. The little finger had risen and expanded, like a lump of bread dough – only it wasn't pale and white, it was mauve and mottled. More like a raw sausage. It wouldn't move, and it seemed to throb, pink and white, pink and white, in time with my heart.

'Mum?' I asked, tentatively, holding up my hand so she could see it.

'Why do you let him get away with it, Katie?' Nan grumbled, ignoring me.

'Why? *Why?* Who else is going to pay the rent?'

'Mum?'

'Shut up, Janet, can't you see we're talking?' Nan shot a hot glare at me before turning her attention back to Mum.

'Go on,' Mum was saying. 'Tell me, I said. Who's going to pay the rent?'

'There's always other options.'

'That's not what you said in your day, if my memory serves me.'

'Divorced him in the end though, didn't I?'

'After we'd all left home and you were left to deal with him on your own, or had you forgotten that part?'

Nan didn't reply. She picked up the kettle and prised off the white plastic lid.

'Have to get a new one soon,' she mumbled, examining the contents with a tight frown.

She turned towards the sink and twisted

the cold tap. A stream of water trickled down.

'This one's scaling up. It's had it.'

'There's a murderer out there!' Mum suddenly cried.

Nan kept her face towards the window, hiding a tired, wary smile.

'Come on, Katie Jane,' she said, gently. 'It's not *Coronation Street*.'

'Well, there is, isn't there? Those two girls–'

'Probably not even linked.'

'But–'

'Oh, Katie, for Christ's sake, this isn't the first time that there's been murders round this way. There's one every other bloody month.'

'But–'

'She was a prostitute, that one they found earlier, did you hear that? Had it coming. And as for that Amber, well, I don't like to speak ill of the dead but from what I gather...'

Nan rolled her eyes, feebly attempting a bit of humour, but she couldn't stop a flash of worry briefly puckering her face. The lines between her eyebrows deepened.

'Headstrong, that boy. Always said it – just like his father.'

'He's only a baby! What's he going to do out there at night, all by himself?'

'We'll have to call the police.'

Mum laughed. 'Look,' she said, tilting her head up so that the bruises hit the full glare of the overhead tube of light, which flickered gently on and off – almost as though it wanted to go to sleep itself — on the ceiling tiles. The tiles were yellowing, just like ours.

'All right. Enough said.'

Shaking her head in disapproval, Nan added another teaspoon of sugar to her tea.

She stood, stirring it around and around.

'We'll wait till morning,' she eventually reasoned. 'You'll be a bit less swollen by then.'

'Mum!'

A teardrop tumbled into my lap. I let out a sob.

'Janet, I'm warning you!'

'He'll be back by morning anyhow, you wait and see,' Nan continued, although I saw her hand brush briefly against the kitchen surface. Touch wood.

Momentarily distracted, I wondered where he was. In a warm caravan, eating toffee apples and candyfloss and speaking to ladies who owned crystal balls. Probably miles away. He'd get to have free goes on fairground rides every day. He'd have all the rides to himself when it was quiet – the waltzers, helter skelters and dodgems, all of them. I pictured him spinning round and round by himself on the twisters, his hair flying about in the generated wind and his head thrown back with the pressure; slowly circling in the big wheel, reclining in a scarlet carriage as it curved a languorous journey through a blue sky, like the colour of his eyes.

I wondered what I'd do if he never came back. I looked back down at my disfigured hand. I couldn't tell them where he was, I'd promised. The finger in front of me throbbed: pink and white, pink and white. Overhead the midnight hour ticked and tocked, and tears began to flow into the seconds, thick and fast. I was tired. The lump in my throat was too big. Strange strangulated whimpers heaved themselves up from my insides, and the room blurred in and out of a watery mist.

Mum's eyes remained downcast and oblivious.

Nan looked up at the noise I was making. A sharp rebuttal hovered on the tip of her tongue, but then she suddenly caught sight of my pantomime limb and her face paled.

'*Jesus Christ,*' she breathed. She slammed her mug down on the side and hurried over, yanking my arm into the light.

'The bloody bastard's gone and broken her finger,' she cried. 'Katherine, stop feeling sorry for yourself and get me a cold cloth, *now.*'

11

They watched through the net curtains as the police car drew up and parked on the side of the road, opposite the house.

'Catch sight of her and they'll have the Social Services round here faster than you can blink,' Nan muttered, her eyes fixed on the two men as they locked the car doors. 'I'm surprised the doctor didn't say anything, as it is.'

'They said they were going to be an hour. I was going to take her over to Net's.'

'Too late now.'

They glanced at each other, their faces white and strained from lack of sleep. Nan had come round first thing and taken me up the doctor's surgery, so that they didn't see Mum and put two and two together.

'What about him upstairs?'

'Leave him to sleep it off, if I were you.'

'He wasn't in till past two,' Mum said. She was panicking. Her swollen lips wobbled and her hands shook as she grabbed my arm and thrust me towards the kitchen door. 'I'll send her up with him. Go on – upstairs, in the bedroom.'

'No,' Nan stopped her. 'You know what he'll be like if she wakes him up.'

They stood very still, thinking, the air heavy with trepidation. I rubbed the patch of arm where Mum's fingers had been.

Suddenly Nan B's face lit up, and she poked an impatient finger towards the cupboard under the stairs, opposite the kitchen window.

'In there,' she growled at me.

I frowned. The cupboard was full of old, dirty rags. It was a dark, soggy closet, where we kept neglected toys and unwanted household things. It was smelly and messy, higgledy-piggledy, like a piece of Aunty Net's world in our own. Mum liked to tell us how she had been brought up on rations. She'd never seen a banana until she was five, she told us, and, because of that, she couldn't bear to be wasteful and throw things away. 'Waste not, want not,' she said. Instead, the useless and never used were stashed away in the cupboard – dirty mops, rotting brooms, little tins of food that we would never eat. Her nuclear war stash, she called it, and it was hard to tell whether she really believed that the motley assortment of rusty mandarins, briny hotdogs and cream crackers really would keep us alive in the event of an apocalyptic emergency. She said that we needed it anyway, just in case – especially after the Falklands last year, and what with never knowing what Maggie or the Russians would get up to next.

'I don't want to,' I said, pouting.

I felt tired and tetchy. Really I just wanted to go to sleep.

'Come on, love, only for a few minutes.'

'Don't want to.'

Mum paused, looking. anxiously out of the window, as the policemen walked over the grass.

'I'll get you some ice cream later,' she bargained. A sharp plea cut through the placatory tones. There were charcoal smudges beneath her eyes, which sparkled from crying, and her normally careworn, nicotine-creased face looked even more haggard than usual. There was something more written over it, that day, than normal worry. Something desperate.

'Bloody ice cream,' Nan snapped, pushing past Mum and swinging me sharply towards the cupboard door. 'You get in there right now, or the only thing you'll be getting is the back of my hand.'

The doorbell rang as she snapped the door shut, and the peeling white paint was eclipsed with shadow.

It was dark, aside from a thin thread of white light beneath the door. The floor was wooden, soft from the damp, with tiny splinters of wood prickling up from the old boards. They scratched through my skirt and into my thighs. I settled down as well as I could, pushing broom handles softly to one side. Something sharp pricked into my back as I leaned against the wall. I jumped up, and felt tentatively through the dark towards it. An old, gritty nail, sticking out from the plaster. Covered with rust.

I sat forward, wrapping my arms around my legs. My freshly bandaged finger felt clumsy, tight. My lungs filled up with stuffy, stale air, as I drifted in and out from the movements and conversation.

'A fall, did you say, Mrs Roberts?'

'I just want to get this clear. You say you tripped over a kerb on your way home from the shops?'

'You tripped?'

Two voices; one gruff and impatient, the other kinder, with a local accent more like our own.

'You deaf?' Mum, at last, snapping nervously.

'Is that right, Mrs Roberts?'

'That's right.'

'Come on, love, we weren't born yesterday. You can't get those bruises from tripping over a kerb.'

The pause was broken only by the habitual rattle of Mum's cough. I visualized the policemen, their uniforms: silver buttons shining, the black material pristinely ironed. Their lips: curved into knowing smiles or exasperated frowns. Raised eyebrows, just one cocked, superior like Captain Spock's. And Mum, framed in the window, backed up against the kitchen counter like a cornered fox, hesitating and biting anxiously on her lips.

I wriggled tentatively, trying to get comfortable without making a sound. The damp seeped up from the wooden boards, into the back of my skirt. In the daylight you could see the stains on the boards. It was a sly, creeping dankness, the type that caused bronchitis and pneumonia and put old, poor people in bed. The mustiness was overpowering. I could almost feel the metallic orange particles hanging in the air. I began to itch, imagining the rust crawling around my legs. The cold plastic of something – an old doll, it felt like – banged against my knee. I knocked it to one side. It thumped, too loud, onto the ground.

Nobody seemed to hear.

'Well?'

Mum still didn't answer. I knew what she was thinking. 'They'll take them away,' Nan had said, last night, speaking in hushed tones. She'd assumed I was asleep, curled up on her living-room sofa, on Mum's lap. The Social Services, she meant. Like they had with Aunty Net's children. 'You'll have to say you fell over.'

Mum cleared her throat. Goosebumps rippled over my arms.

'I–' Mum began, but then Nan's fractious voice sliced through the air.

'Stranger things have happened than a woman falling over a kerb,' she snapped. 'Anyhow, we didn't ring you so you could come and pass the time of day about my daughter having a fall.'

'We're trying to establish why your son – your grandson – might have decided to run away. These are questions we need to ask.'

'I'm not standing here asking you questions about your private life, am I?'

'It's not his son that's disappeared, love.'

And the other one, again: 'It would be far more helpful for James if you were frank with us, Mrs Roberts. We've encountered this type of incident many times in the past, we're here to help you.'

'And what type of incident would that be?'

'I was talking to your daughter.'

'And I was talking to you.'

There was a pause, and then they changed tack.

'You've got a young girl, you say?'

'That's right,' Mum said. 'Janet. She's eight, she'll be nine in October.'

'Where's she today?'

'She's gone into town with her aunty.' It was Nan again, stepping in before Mum had chance to reply. 'It didn't seem right keeping her here, what with all this palaver.'

I thought of Amber Jenkins's coffin. She'd been buried last week, but Mum hadn't been well enough to take us to the funeral. It was morbid to go, anyway, she'd said, though she'd happily listened to all of the details when Nan came back from it: who was there, what they were wearing, how they were looking, what was being said. But it didn't really matter what was being said, I thought, because whichever way you went about it she was still dead. I pictured her underground: kind of asleep but not asleep. I wondered whether the air was as black, as soggy with life as it was in this cupboard. Whether it was as rotten. Worms. There would be worms in her grave; they'd eat through the coffin and into her body. Wet, writhing worms, blind in the darkness. And black bruises crawling slowly, over her skin.

I shivered, and curled a strand of hair around my good fingers, bringing it up to my mouth, sucking the follicles. My mouth filled with dirty saliva.

Nan didn't like me sucking my hair. She said she'd known of little girls who'd died from all the germs.

'You just boiled this, Katie?' Nan's voice broke through another lull in the conversation.

'Mmm,' Mum replied.

'There's not enough water in it. Move

over, I'll fill it up.' I pictured them, standing with their backs to the officers, facing the kettle and the window, each seemingly engrossed in their immediate tasks.

One of the men cleared his throat to speak, but Nan quickly cut him off.

'Tea?' she asked.

Ten minutes later and all of their questions had been dispensed with.

'Is that it then?' Mum asked, helplessly.

'Listen, love, don't worry.' The kinder voice spoke. 'It's not unusual for boys that age to up and off on a little adventure of their own. Chances are that he'll be back within the day. That's what usually happens.'

Receiving no response – I could hear Mum crying again – he must have turned to Nan.

'Nice to have met you,' he said.

'You too, you too,' Nan answered, but her tone was grudging.

'Oh, and Mrs Roberts?'

'*Mrs Bainbridge,* thank you very much.'

'I'm sorry – Mrs Bainbridge.'

'Yes?'

'When Mr Roberts gets back from work, ask him to keep an eye on his family, so that they don't go falling over any more kerbs. And just in case he forgets, remind him that we'll be popping over in the next couple of days.'

'It's just a waiting game, love,' the kind one added. 'I'm sure he'll be back soon. If he's not – I'm sure he will be, mind you – we'll get together and have a rethink.'

Nan said nothing. After a while I heard the door slam shut.

Footsteps approached the cupboard, the handle twisted noisily and the door swung open. Bright light swept over me. Amber Jenkins faded; the contents of the cupboard turned back – from horrible, nightmarish things – into everyday objects: paint tins, a dusty broom, a cluster of abandoned toys.

Nan stood, enveloped in daylight; smoke snaked up from the B&H in her mouth and her angry eyes glinted through her glasses.

I blinked up at her.

'Mrs Roberts,' she snarled to herself in disgust, pulling me up from the floor and dusting me down. Mum stood crying, in the background. 'Calling me *Mrs Roberts*. The shame of it.'

12

Later that Monday Dick Roberts stood, his face bowed as he mixed the soluble tablet and water that Mum had handed to him. The cloudy liquid swirled round and round in the tumbler, and the only sound in the room was the fizz and pop of the bubbles as they cracked against the surface of the water – that, and the rattle of the teaspoon against glass.

No one looked at each other.

Mum and Nan sat at the dinner table, wordlessly sucking in cigarettes. Nan's eyes fixed disdainfully on some point in the distance: a blade of grass through the window and right at the opposite end of the sports field, two women talking, a solitary man walking his dog. Mum's eyes were downcast, puffy from crying. She fumbled nervously with the dull gold band clamped around her wedding finger. I looked down at my own fingers. The bandage hadn't even been on for a day and the edges were already fringed with black dirt.

He was ready for work, dressed in the same royal blue overalls that everyone at the car factory wore. He worked on the assembly line where they spray-painted the bodies of the cars, and his overalls always returned home splattered with a new rainbow of stains.

Other than those unavoidable blotches of paint they were pristine. Mum took the same care with those uniforms that she took with everything else, washing and ironing them until the collars were as straight as those on a sombre funeral suit. Aunty Net said that Mum must have been the only woman on the estate that bothered to starch bloody factory overalls.

'Christ, I can't even be bothered with my normal clothes,' she laughed.

Dick Roberts didn't belong in the kitchen, even at the best of times. It was Mum and Nan's, not his. When he was there he seemed to lurk in it, an unwelcome interloper, like a furtive hyena on the periphery of a lion's den. He was weak in the kitchen. He could cause a scene but he didn't have much control. Talk died whenever he entered the room, and half-finished conversations hung subversively in the air, mingling with the cigarette fog.

It made him angry, the quiet, censorious aura that rubbed up against him whenever he entered. You could gauge it on his face, even when it was expressionless. Waves of it swept out from his body, a hot sweat ready to catch fire.

It was palpable that Monday afternoon. He was angry with Mum, he was angry with all of us for the throb of blame that knocked against his sense of reason. He didn't look at us. He stood by the cooker with his back to us, sipping his drink and gazing stonily out of the window, watching his workmates walk by. They were the nightshift, and they could be seen every evening of the week, long lines of melancholy blue, walking the half-mile to work with the same dogged slouch that we wore to school.

The hungover pallor of his skin illuminated his freckles, which flashed over him, shining red, a burning mass of fiery constellations.

After a minute or two he moved over to the sink and, dropping the glass into it with a rebellious clatter, turned and stooped to pick up his work holdall.

He paused, awkward.

'Phone the supervisor's office if there's any news,' he said gruffly, and then was gone.

13

Nan B hated the Robertses. There was bad history between them. That much was sure, but not much more. It was an elusive history, one full of half-finished sentences, raised eyebrows and pregnant pauses. All I knew was that Nan B hated the Robertses, and that she wasn't one to give up a grudge. That, and what happened a couple of years back.

It started like this.

One late Thursday afternoon, Nan B, who had been surprisingly absent all week, came around to our house. She didn't let herself in, like she usually did, but instead rapped curtly on the window and stood waiting beside the front door. We looked up from our colouring books and saw her framed outline against the kitchen window. She was in her beige Sunday coat and had her best pink chiffon scarf tied over her hair, even though it was only a weeknight. The net curtains scattered lace snowflakes over her face and it was difficult to gauge her expression, though her tone of voice soon settled that.

'Well, aren't you going to offer me a cuppa?' we heard her snapping in the hall, after Mum had let her in.

Hovering in the kitchen doorway, she glared around the room, her eyes resting briefly on us before she switched her attention back to Mum, who had hurried back into the kitchen and was standing by the cooker, watching her.

'If my daughter can't even offer me a cup of tea...' she complained in a staged whisper, taking a dramatic step backwards.

Mum started at the complaint, and quickly turned towards the kettle.

'Hold your horses, hold your horses,' she said. 'I was just about to make you one.'

'No, don't bother,' Nan replied, shaking her head. 'If you haven't got the time to make a cup of tea for your poor mother don't worry – I can always go and get one from my other daughter.'

'Oh, Mum, don't be like that,' Mum said, helplessly, reddening as she plucked a mug from the cupboard and gestured Nan towards a chair.

Nan didn't reply, but she did sit down. She slowly began to unpin the scarf from her hair. Her pink chiffon scarf, her favourite.

She enjoyed telling us how it perfectly matched every single item of her wardrobe, which were mainly dresses from the forties and fifties (her clothes, like her thoughts and anecdotes for most of the time, remained in the decades she loved best). They were pastel affairs with coy collars and matching belts, dresses that she'd cover up indoors with a blue chequered pinafore, so as not to get them stained. By the time she wore the pink chiffon scarf to our house that Thursday afternoon, she'd had it for years, and the soft rosebud material was so old that tiny, translucent brown spots crawled up from each corner. They matched the liver spots on Nan's hands. Its ageing fragility didn't bother her. In fact, it only seemed to add to its preciousness, because she knew the number of times she'd be able to wear it were limited.

James and I stopped colouring, and watched the situation with interest. Mum and Nan hardly ever rowed. They bickered, about Mum's bad cooking and television shows and over certain details in family anecdotes – was the dress blue, or red, had it been 1964 or 1965? – but that was it. Nothing more than that. 'Thick as thieves,' Aunty Net always said of them, and it was true. This was different. The pink scarf was involved and the tones were fraught, not affectionately irritated. There was something guilty in Mum's posture and something accusatory in Nan's – though that was naturally the way with Nan, she always had God on her side. Their movements seemed heavy, premeditated, like something had been brewing.

After folding it into neat quarters, Nan snapped open her handbag and placed the scarf safely in it. Then she let out a sigh, and scowled down into the tea Mum had placed on a coaster for her.

'Gnat's pee,' she grunted. Holding the mug up to her lips with a slight grimace, she took a dainty sip. She held the liquid in her mouth and, with a sour expression, swallowed.

'I take two sugars in my tea,' she announced, thrusting the mug back in Mum's direction. 'Not seen me for five days and you've already forgotten how I like it.'

'It has got two sugars in it,' Mum protested – then, reconciliatory: 'Do you want another one?'

'No, don't bother.'

Mum took the mug and turned on the hot water, squirting washing-up liquid into the bowl.

'Why can't you wait till after dinner, eh? No wonder your bills are so high.'

Nan didn't say any more. Mum turned the taps off and dropped the mug into the water, but she didn't wash it. Resting her elbows on the draining board, she peered out at the road through the semi-circle at the bottom of the net curtains.

Ten minutes must have passed, and the silence might have gone on for hours if it hadn't been that Mum, suddenly impatient, turned and reproached Nan.

'Honestly, Mum,' she cried. 'You're kicking up a stink over nothing. You don't even know them.'

James nudged me, wrinkling his forehead. *Who?* he mouthed.

I shrugged.

Nan sat, staring Mum out for a bit before she answered. She could make a scene, Nan, when she wanted to.

'I know that a man doesn't lose contact with his family for twenty years without there being a reason,' she said.

She didn't shout, but her voice was so low that Mum, expert through years of experience in the many different nuances of Nan's tone, flinched.

'It's only for the weekend,' she whimpered,

from her corner.

'I don't care. One Roberts is already one too many. Nan stood up and assessed Mum for a few moments, before voicing the ultimatum she had obviously come around to deliver. 'So you're definitely going then?'

'Put a lid on that felt-tip,' Mum said to James, briefly distracted as her eyes drifted to where we sat. 'You'll get ink all over the carpet.'

Then, gathering some final grains of strength, she straightened her back and made a surprisingly defiant reply to Nan's question.

'Yes,' she said.

That was that. Nan B's temper snapped. She picked up the cream handbag and, clicking the gold clasp shut, strode out through the hall.

'Well, I won't be stopping then,' she snarled. The front door banged open.

'Don't come crying to me when it all goes to pot,' she shouted, and with a loud slam, banged it shut.

We watched as she disappeared up the garden path and through the gate. Mum stood motionless beside the kitchen door-way, a tea towel hanging limply in her hand.

'Storm in a teacup,' she said, talking to

119

herself, softly shaking her head. 'I don't know, silly old cow.'

'Why's Nan upset?' James asked.

Mum glanced down at him – well, more beyond him, really. She shrugged and picked up a plate to dry.

'I suppose you might as well know,' she said. 'We're off to the seaside.'

'The seaside?' James repeated.

We cast puzzled glances at each other. We'd never been on holiday before. We couldn't afford it, Mum always said whenever we asked her, and we didn't dare ask Dick Roberts at all.

'On holiday?' I picked up a red colouring pencil, brought it up to my mouth, and began to chew ponderously.

It was an odd idea, surreal. A family holiday. They were events full of ice creams and smiles.

'Don't do that!' Mum yanked the pencil out from my lips and cuffed the back of my head. But, even though she'd just been rowing with Nan B, she couldn't help but give a small smile. 'You'll have to have next Friday off school. We're going up to see your dad's family. You've got another nan, you know, and a grampy too.'

This was news to us.

'How come we've never seen them?' James pried. 'I didn't know we had another family.'

Mum looked as though he had asked her a tricky question.

'Never mind that,' was all she eventually said.

'What will we have to call them?'

'Nan and Grampy, you silly idiot, what else do you think?' she said, frowning in irritation. 'We're going up there anyhow and it's the first time that your dad's seen them in years so you'd better bloody well behave yourselves.'

With that she had turned pointedly back towards the sink, and, lighting up a cigarette, stared out of the window in a hazy silence, cutting our enquiries short.

14

Monday melted into Tuesday, the day ticked warily into night.

James hadn't come back. Two whole nights he'd been gone, much longer than I supposed he'd be away for. Mum and Nan racked their brains, trying to figure out just where he was, but to them it remained a nightmarish mystery: he'd vanished – like a magic trick, into thin air.

I didn't know what Dick Roberts made of it. If he felt anything at all he kept it quiet. He came back from work and slept throughout Tuesday morning, waking in the early afternoon. He put on his clothes then, refusing the lunch that Nan had prepared, disappearing to take a look around the estate. But he didn't say anything to Mum or me.

It was Mum who was the worry. Nan tried to keep her buoyed up, but she couldn't bear it. If she looked ill before, she was like a zombie now. It was as if her resistance to everything had caved in and when she wasn't hacking up phlegm – and phlegm that had now turned bloody – she was on the phone to Cowley police station. She rang them fifteen, twenty times through the Monday and Tuesday, unable to contain herself as the minutes ticked viciously on and on, with no sign of her son. At last they had told her not to ring until the following day, that they were looking around the estate and up in town, and if there was any news they'd phone. 'You don't give a flying fuck, do you?' she had screamed into the mouthpiece. 'It's just one less little estate fucker to worry about for you, isn't it?' She would have gone on, but Nan wrestled the phone off her, hastily apologizing before she hung up. ('I'm sorry,' she'd said. 'She's a bit run down.')

There wasn't anything to do – except wait, and go to bed. It was then, in the dark, that the pictures in my head got brighter. They were all right during the day, like an over-exposed photograph they lost their definitions, but alone in my room at night they took on dimensions larger than life.

James replacing Amber Jenkins in the ditch. Slowly swinging from side to side in the soupy mud, eyes facing heaven and a necklace of blue bruises around his neck, a green nettle leaf stuck to his pallid, dirt-flecked skin.

James with the fairground people, plucking free tokens from his pocket and playing in an arcade. He wins a game, and shiny silver pieces cascade down into the slot, so many that soon it is overflowing and the coins are clattering down around his feet.

With the magic gypsy people, dressed in rainbow clothes and peering into a crystal globe, seeing a new family that does not contain me.

The bedroom felt empty, with just me in it.

The dialogue from a television drama drifted upstairs from the living room. There was nobody in there. Dick Roberts had left for work hours before. Nan had popped home to water her plants. Mum, I knew, was curled up in the hallway by the phone, her frayed dressing gown wrapped around her, drifting in and out of fretful sleep. She must have turned up the volume for company.

15

'Go on, have a look,' Grampy R had said, winking at us as he crouched down.

We sat up in the sleeping bags Mum had brought us especially, and looked uncertainly at the tiny stranger kneeling beside us.

'Go on, under the pillow,' he smiled. His eyes were blue, the same colour as Dick Roberts's. The whites were pink around the edges, and a small tear seemed perpetually to hang in the ducts, waiting to fall, but they sparkled kindly.

Lying on the thin cotton sheet, beneath our

pillows, were two shiny fifty-pence pieces.

'It's from the fairies,' Grampy R whispered conspiratorially. 'They give presents to children who are very good.'

He pulled himself up from the palsied carpet and, wheezing a little, turned away from us and tiptoed over to the big double bed where Mum and Dick Roberts lay sleeping on the other side of the room, placing mugs on the bedside table. It was a big room, ramshackle with mismatched, dilapidated furniture. A door to an old oak wardrobe swung ajar, a print of galloping white horses hung lopsided on the flower-papered walls and an ancient sofa sat to the right of the bed, sagging in the middle. A breeze rattled through the window panes, one of which had been broken and covered ineptly with cardboard from a Walkers crisp box. The morning air stung my nose.

Mum opened her eyes as Grampy R approached the bed. She looked wildly around her for a second, as though she wasn't quite sure where she was and then, coming to, started to pull herself up from the pillow. He stopped her with a wave of his hand.

'No rush,' he said. 'You get some rest, and I'll make the litt'luns some breakfast.'

Glancing back over to us and putting his fingers up to his lips, he trod softly back over the room and stood at the door, beckoning, with another wave, for us to follow.

From the far side of the bed Dick Roberts let out a long, gurgling snore.

Grampy and Nan R's flat was a relic from the Victorian slums. It only had two rooms, a living room/kitchen and the bedroom. It nestled around the back of an old-fashioned corner shop that must have competed with it in age. We'd arrived the previous evening. The bus driver had shouted our destination from the front of the number 42 that we'd caught at the train station. We got off, putting our bags down on the pavement and looking around uncertainly. The air smelled mineral, salty. A large seagull squawked overhead. No one walked by. In the distance, at the very far end of the road, and flanked by an old-fashioned promenade, I could see the sea. It was green, broken by frills of white that rolled forward, forward, forward, in hypnotic regularity.

Mum began to fret. We should have brought a map, she said, why hadn't we brought a map? Dick Roberts's eyes had narrowed.

'Don't start,' he warned, and his harsh voice hovered just this side of a threat. He pulled irritably at the brown tie he was wearing and rubbed at the cuffs of his suit jacket as he looked around, examining walls for the right street sign.

At that moment a greying man in white overalls appeared in the shop doorway. He stood, watching our bewildered faces. 'You Ernie and Vera's youngest?' he asked, eventually, squinting suspiciously at our luggage. Putting on the small, perfectly round glasses that he had been cleaning on his apron, he wrinkled his nose at Dick Roberts and broke into a cheerful smile, obviously satisfied his guess had been the right one. 'Recognize a Roberts face anywhere,' he said, and pointed to a dark, graffitied alleyway by the side of the shop. 'They've been expecting you. Round the back.'

The following morning Nan R lay asleep on the living-room sofa. We sat in the stiff chairs opposite her, waiting as Grampy R got breakfast ready. She was big, almost double the size of her husband or any of the Bainbridge family. When she had opened the door last night she had thrown her arms around each of us, in turn, and James had later whispered that he was scared he was going to be sucked into her massive, manky old tits. 'Tits' was his new word that summer, and he liked to practise it whenever he could. Tits. They swayed, pendulous, in the lilac dress she was wearing.

She lay now, covered by a threadbare orange blanket, snoring loudly. Her lips lopped open at one side, an early prophecy of a later stroke, and a thin stream of spit dribbled out from the corner of her mouth.

The living room was similar to the bedroom, scattered with oddments of failing furniture. A coffee table with a splintered leg, a cracked, black-mottled mirror. Mildew climbed the chintz-covered walls, curling up the weathered patterns like ivy, making it hardly distinguishable from the garden outside.

'Porridge all right? Bit of Ready Brek?'

Grampy R shuffled dishes around in the makeshift kitchen, by the front door. It was a wooden sideboard, really, that was all, with a cracked Victorian washbasin. They didn't have a fridge, only a larder, and all of the cooking was done on a small hob placed on an old, crocked Welsh dresser. They had an outside toilet and once a week, on a Thursday, Nan and Grampy heated up a basin full of water and had a wash. That's what they had told Mum and Dick Roberts the evening before. They cleaned their teeth in the kitchen sink every Thursday too. They would have liked to clean them more often but toothpaste was an expensive commodity and their teeth – probably because they were false by now, and less susceptible to rotting – seemed to get by.

'Do you remember in the old days, Ernie?' Nan R had shouted across the room. She was deaf, and her voice rolled out in a steady, well-practised boom. Everyone had to pitch their voices so she could hear the conversation, and it made the already uneasy reunion all the more self-conscious as Dick Roberts and Mum struggled to make themselves heard. 'Do you remember when we used to clean them with coal?'

She laughed at the memory, until the sound broke and fragmented into a fit of coughs, which she rattled into a grey handkerchief. Beside me, on the floor, James wrinkled his nose.

It had been strange, that previous evening. It was almost like being on a stage set, with two different performances colliding. The four of us, all starched clothes and tortured smiles, mouthing the script of a happy

nuclear quartet while they, an old, im-
poverished couple, took their bows and
desperately tried to hide the squalor of their
existence behind cheap pink lipstick and a
clumsy veneer of cheer. That, and trying to
ignore what they must have all been
thinking about: the difficult bridge of a
runaway child and twenty-odd years.

'How long have you lived here, then?'
Mum had asked, tentatively. She glanced
around her, clutching her mug of tea
between scarlet nails, sitting nervously
upright on the frayed chair, as she tried not
to notice the peeling wallpaper and the webs
of mildew.

'Eh?'

'How long you been here?'

'You what?'

Mum's resolution started to falter.

'H-how long—'

'Can't hear, love. Wait a second, I'll turn
my hearing aid up.'

Bending over, her lilaced breasts flopping
onto her knees, Nan R began to fiddle with
the ugly plastic object that protruded from
her left ear.

'She wants to know, Vera, how long it is
we've—'

'Hold your horses, Ernie, can't you see

I'm doing something?'

'Don't worry, I was only asking–'

The conversation, which had been getting louder and louder with each new sentence, trailed off into silence. Everyone sat, watching the purple lumps of Nan R's hunched frame as she wrestled with the hearing aid. Dick Roberts twitched uncomfortably. It was hard to tell what was more difficult for him: chit-chatting with parents as though he'd last spoken to them yesterday, or sustaining a show of affection for us.

'Buggered, this thing,' Nan R shouted, her loud voice muffled in the folds of her dress. 'I'll have it right in a minute.'

In lieu of his wife's response, Grampy R, who had hardly spoken, turned towards Mum, taking in the discomfiture on her face. Abashed, he raised himself uneasily from the armchair he was sitting in. His eyes trailed the room, assessing what she saw, what he had long been used to, before he cleared his throat to speak.

'Must be getting on five years now, I'd say,' he answered, hesitantly, throwing her an embarrassed, reassuring smile. 'It's not as bad as it looks, is it, Vera? We get by.'

'Eh?'

Mum blushed, casting a furtive, nervous glance towards Dick Roberts before looking down at her feet.

'Oh no, I wasn't saying ... it's – it's lovely, honest.'

'Don't pester them, Katherine,' Dick Roberts snapped, throwing her an angry frown.

Mum reddened, biting her lips. She pulled her pretend fur coat further around her shoulders. I looked down at her feet, which were by my side. Taupe nylon tights and snowy stilettos, scuffed at the points, with tiny stars of brown winking through the peeling white. They had made her totter unsteadily along the station platform, earlier, when we'd first arrived. She'd struggled to keep up and had stopped a few times, pausing to catch deep breaths of the salty, fish and chip breezes.

A string of cerise sores crawled along her hairline, from the perm she'd had done especially.

Dick Roberts sat, uncomfortably straight in his grey suit, his face taut with tension. Grampy R sat on the opposite chair. Occasionally his eyes met ours, or his son's, and awkward smiles broke the line of his lips. A plate of cake sat uneaten on the decrepit coffee table.

'Well, twenty years,' Grampy R suddenly said, struggling to open up the conversation and stumbling, inadvertently, into the taboo subject. ('Don't mention it,' Dick Roberts had threatened Mum on the train. 'I don't want any of that rubbish brought up.') 'It's been twenty years, can you imagine? When I last saw you, you were nothing but a teenage nipper in school clothes.'

He paused, looking us over as a flash of sadness crossed his wrinkled face.

'And now – now you've got a lovely wife and daughter, and a son who's the spit of you,' he finished, his voice floundering and breaking off.

I glanced at James, who didn't look thrilled at the comparison, and then at Dick Roberts. His pale fingers touched his tie and fluttered up to his face, as his eyes nervously scanned the ceiling. He didn't reply.

Mum wriggled uncomfortably in her seat. Her lips opened and shut as she hunted for something to break the tension.

'We could – we could wash that graffiti in the alleyway down for you, tomorrow, if you like?'

'For Christ's sake, Katherine, stop making a fuss!'

Grampy R's face flushed.

'Don't worry, it's fine,' he began, but at that moment Nan R lurched upwards, flashing a wide, sunny grin as she straightened herself.

'There we are,' she said, still shouting. 'Bloody NHS, nothing ever works.'

She beamed and, leaning over, picked up a slice of the cake.

'We'll go down the beach tomorrow,' she said, winking at James and me as she sprayed ginger coloured crumbs towards our feet. 'Build a few sandcastles, have a bit of ice cream, howsabout that?'

Dick Roberts, pink with his momentary burst of temper, forced a smile and, reaching down, inexpertly patted our heads.

'That'd be lovely,' he said.

'Eh?'

16

Wednesday. Just after lunch Aunty Net hurried down the garden path and burst in through the front door waving a newspaper excitedly above her head. An arid, rotten scent wafted out around her, as she tottered over the kitchen carpet.

'They've got an artist's impression!' she shouted importantly, oblivious to Nan's discouraging frowns.

'Shh!' Nan snapped, looking her up and down and pointedly sniffing the air before averting her eyes in repugnance. 'You'll wake everyone up.'

Aunty Net took no notice. She banged her tattered handbag down onto the kitchen table, in front of Nan, and spread the newspaper across the surface, riffling noisily through the pages, pausing only to stifle a fetid burp. Nan winced. She did smell a bit, Aunty Net. At such close range I could see brown stains covering her navy-blue mac.

'Where the bugger has it disappeared to, then?' Aunty Net puzzled as she reached the back page. She sighed and licked her fingers, flipping the *Oxford Mail* back over onto its front. She had half turned the first page and was preparing to repeat the whole process when she suddenly spotted the article that she was after.

'Look, front page!' she cried breathlessly, jabbing the paper with her finger. She beamed up around the room, her eyes not quite meeting ours. The burst capillaries over her cheeks seemed especially blotchy;

they stood out like fragile, proud poppies on her otherwise wretchedly pale, thin skin.

It was the booze that did it, Nan said. It was wasting her away. And it did seem that the more she drank, the more her already frail frame appeared, in inverse correspondence, to wither and shrink. It wasn't just her height, either. Bits and pieces of her seemed to fall off, through the years. She was attacked by the same condition as Mum, and psoriasis caused skin to flake off her body in thick, dry clumps. Occasional teeth fell out, here and there, lending her smile a comic-strip gappiness until she had new false ones put in. They were almost as bad; their artificial glare threw the yellow ones into such vivid relief that sometimes it seemed that Aunty Net was wearing a stripy winter scarf inside her mouth. The whites of her eyes floundered in a flush of pink and her ratty dark hair had thinned so much that albino patches of scalp shone through the black.

Nan snatched the newspaper from the table, ignoring Aunty Net's jubilation as she adjusted her glasses and stretched it out, in front of her.

'Look at you,' she hissed, while she squinted at the paper. 'Three o'clock in the afternoon and look at the state of you.'

And then: 'Coming round here, shouting the house down, as though Katie hasn't got enough on her plate. And you haven't even got the decency to ask after your own nephew.'

'He back yet?'

'What does it look like, you bloody fool?'

'I don't know why you're making such a fuss. My little devils used to run off the whole time.'

'And look what happened to them, eh? Anyway, don't you change the subject, always steering the bloody conversation back to yourself – you come round here, spouting off about things like this, as if Katie really wants to know what's going on outside on the streets...' Nan continued to scan the page. I watched her eyes flicker from line to line. 'She'll have a bloody heart attack if she sees this.'

'Six foot, they say – do you see that? Lindsay Hamish spotted him with that girl a couple of hours before they found her–'

'*Shh, I said!* Katie'll hear you!'

'Where is she, anyway?'

Nan didn't reply. She finished reading and slapped the newspaper down onto the kitchen table. Casting her hands over her chequered pinafore, she pulled herself up from her chair and fixed Aunty Net with one of her glacial stares before grabbing her elbow and propelling her back in the direction of the front door.

'What are you doing?'

'Sending you home.'

'What do you want to do that for?'

'Do you think I was born yesterday?'

'I—'

'Think a couple of Polos are going to fool me?'

They disappeared through the hallway.

'I'm not having you coming round here upsetting everyone,' I could hear Nan saying, as the door clicked open.

'Where's Kate, anyway?'

'In bed, having a rest before the police appear.'

An instant later Nan reappeared in the kitchen, without Aunty Net, who was in the garden and banging her fists on the kitchen window. She pressed her blistered cheeks against the cool pane and squinted indignantly through the netting.

'Give me back my newspaper,' she complained. 'That cost me sixteen pee.'

But Nan just walked over to the sink and pulled the blind down on her.

'Bloody disgrace,' she muttered, repositioning herself at the table and picking up the newspaper for a more leisurely look.

I could just about see the page she was reading. The writing was too small, but a bold, definite face stared out at me. It was an artist's impression of a dishevelled, dark-haired man. A thick jaw with a three-day stubble, an unsmiling face. So that was what he looked like.

Mum had only managed the morning downstairs. She trailed despondently down to the kitchen in her pink dressing gown at around nine o'clock, long after she usually got up. She didn't respond to Nan's attempts at light-hearted conversation, and left her morning cup of tea untouched. She had a bad feeling, she kept repeating, propped over the table with her hands half covering her face. Three days and he still wasn't back. Three days. She couldn't understand it – a kid of that age didn't disappear for that long without there being something wrong. And look at the police, doing nothing – *nothing* – about it.

'Well, Katie,' Nan had said. 'What do you expect? Look at this murder business. If they can't even muster the energy to sort that out, do you really think they're going to bother with a runaway? They must get a dozen kiddies legging it every week, up this way.'

But Mum had started to cry at the mention of murder, and so Nan shut up.

'I wish you'd stop grizzling,' was all she said. 'You're worse than a bloody baby.'

Mum brushed her aside, telling her to piss off home if she didn't want to put up with it. After hovering tearfully by the window for a couple of hours, whipping up the nets at the sight of any small blond boy, she retreated back upstairs.

'I'll sleep in the spare bed,' she said, looking pale. 'You don't mind, do you?'

It was the bed that Nan always slept in when she stayed over, in the small bedroom at the back of the house. Dick Roberts was asleep in Mum's room.

'Get some rest,' Nan said. 'You don't look well. I'll hold the fort, I'll wake you when the police get here.'

'And if anyone rings?'

Nan nodded, but Mum still hesitated before leaving.

'Why aren't they doing anything more?' she started again, her voice veering dangerously between gravel and high whine. 'If it were one of their kids it'd be all over the newspapers by now.

'Come on, Katie. It happens all the time — I just said so. Remember when Terry disappeared? Frightened the life out of me, the little devil. You'll just have to wait, like everyone else.'

'But *three* days, Mum.'

'Go on, upstairs. You'll feel better after a rest.'

Nan spent the remainder of the morning and afternoon in the kitchen, at the kitchen table beside me, pacing the heavy hours with a crossword. A police car eventually drew up at half six, and she chivvied me up to Mum's bedroom, which still smelled muggy with sleep, with a colouring book and instructions to stay quiet if I knew what was good for me.

The policeman spoke for some time to Mum and Dick and Nan. I could hear bits of what was going on. It just seemed to be a long line of questions, one after another, much more detailed than last time.

Did he take anything with him?

Any money gone?

Was there anyone who he could be staying with, any friends, or relatives?

Was there any specific reason why he'd

want to run away – a fight, an argument?

Could they have a couple more photos, to take away?

And more questions I couldn't make out.

Then one of the policemen started saying something about a reason that they had to believe, and his voice dipped out of hearing. The next thing I heard was Mum's voice, raised in distress.

'No, no social workers,' she cried.

Someone broke in to quieten her but her voice rose all the more.

'Sticking their nose in where it doesn't belong. I saw what they did to my sister. Mum? Tell them. Tell them it broke Net's heart. Mum!'

It went on, my name mentioned once or twice: that they needed to talk to me too, and how did we get on – James and I – and would he have told me where he was going? Until, at last, they left – saying, louder as they walked through the hallway, that it was unfortunate, and a worry, but boys will be boys and the only advice they could give at this stage was to try to stay calm and to wait.

Evening came. Nan retrieved an old pack of cards from one of the side drawers, and dealt out the scuffed oblongs for a round of patience. The cards were mismatched, not one pack but a combination of two, and her dealings cast out asymmetrical patterns of red and royal blue. Occasionally she rubbed her hands over her eyes and stood up, craning her neck to look at the clock. Her face had been creased into a frown for the best part of the last few days, and there was a large, impatient gorge running between her eyes. She peered irritably down at the cards, turning over a king, a jack, a dirty, finger-smudged queen.

'You would say, wouldn't you, love?' she asked me, her eyes focused on the one she was turning. It was the ten of clubs. 'You would tell us if you knew where your brother had got to?'

It was the first time she'd spoken in an hour.

I sat opposite her, my feet dangling from the chair, and concentrated on the page in my colouring book.

I knew she'd ask me at some stage, especially after earlier.

'Would you?'

I gave a quick nod.

Red for the toadstool, green for the fairy dress.

'Because ... I know that you're loyal, and

that you wouldn't want to snitch on him, but it's a big wide world out there. It's not safe for an eleven-year-old boy. You know that, don't you?'

I scrambled around in the plastic margarine tub, looking for the right colours.

I'd promised.

He'd never forgive me if I squealed on him, and cut his adventure short.

'Can I have some lemonade, Nan?' I asked.

She stopped playing and looked at me, in a funny way.

'You're a funny girl,' she said, shaking her head. 'If it were anyone else, but with you...'

'Mum always lets me.'

'Go on then, go and get yourself a glass. What are you looking like that for? Don't expect me to do it.'

And with that she turned back to her cards.

I could hear noises from the living room, where Dick Roberts sat. It was his night off, before he changed over to dayshifts. He was on his own. The noise was the television, which veered from tune to tune with his switching of channels. The sounds performed a crazy waltz from one mood to another – one moment an argument from a soap opera, the next instant the even, placid tones of a news presenter. The switching got faster, faster, more and more irritable as the evening wore on.

It was Wednesday, his worst day.

I'd never spent a Wednesday without James before.

I tried not to think about it.

After a while Nan kicked back her chair. She stood up and pressed her hand to her mouth in a dramatic exhibition of a yawn before she walked over to the sideboard and opened one of the cupboard doors.

'Oh dear, oh dear, I don't know,' she said, mumbling to herself as she fumbled through the contents. When her hand reappeared it was holding a small bottle of ginger liquid.

She caught me watching her.

'Little bit of something,' she said, by way of explanation, 'to calm my nerves.'

She poured herself a small glass and the scent filtered through the air. It smelled like Aunty Net.

'Go into the living room,' she said, sitting back down with a sigh. 'Ask your dad if he wants a cup of tea.'

I stared at her in surprise. She'd caught me off guard. Mum would never have asked me to do that. She knew as well as me –

Wednesday, the worst day of the week. Nan knew too, but it must have slipped her mind. She didn't notice the expression on my face. She sat, taking dainty sips out of her tumbler, with her varicosed legs crossed and her head propped in one wrinkled hand. Her eyes were far away, and when she eventually stirred it was to chide me.

'Go on,' she snapped. 'What are you waiting for?'

But we were hardly ever allowed in there, James or I. He said we'd mess it up. He'd kill me if I went in the living room without him calling me first.

I opened my mouth to protest, but nothing came out, it was suddenly dry. I tried to swallow. I looked at my bandaged finger, at the glaring bruises on my arm, and then back at her frowning at me.

I struggled to my feet, turned haltingly, and slowly walked through the kitchen and into the hall where the living-room door stood, slightly ajar a mere three steps away.

Of course it was just a door.

Just a polished plywood door, with four panels and a bronzed metal handle, the sort of door everyone had.

It seemed alive, to me.

The planks of wood menaced and sneered,

the darker knots swirled into leering grimaces. The cake-slice of carpet I could see between it and the living room stood on end, the fibres bristling with hostility.

I could feel his eyes smarting, his hands twitching. I could feel his muscles tensing.

The look of anger on his face.

He was standing behind the door, probably right now. He'd probably heard Nan telling me and he'd thought, I'll catch her, coming in here without my say-so. He was waiting behind the door, fist raised–

'What the bugger are you playing at?' Nan glared down to where I sat cowering on the bottom stair ledge. 'I should have done it myself in the first place, not bloody wasted my breath.'

She disappeared into the living room.

'Kettle's boiled,' I heard her say.

I ran upstairs, slipped on my pyjamas and climbed hurriedly into bed.

17

I was in a place I didn't know, or even understand. It was bruised and tangled; its dimensions seemed to oscillate and the ground beneath me throbbed, like a body in pain. I strained my eyes to see but the dream twisted and turned, ducking away from me.

A nightmarish pantomime of images came at me in sharp flashes. Nan appeared. She looked old, gnarled and rotten, like a churchyard tree. She was clutching a lead and when I looked down it was Mum she was walking. I reached down to touch her and she barked and snapped at my hand. I laughed. The sound rippled out through the treaded air and another familiar voice joined my own. I turned to see and it was James, standing beside me. He was clutching his sides and keeling over, towards the swampish ground. I thought he was laughing at me and then I saw the look of panic on his face and held my hand out to him. He screamed and staggered backwards, falling away from me and disappearing into the mud of our neighbourhood ditch.

I shouted, dropping down onto my knees and groping in the fetid water.

I began to sink, and the more I lifted my feet and scrabbled for the shore, the more I was pulled down. Amber Jenkins appeared from the bushes and grabbed at me with decomposed fingers. She was chanting something, over and over again, but her voice came as if from underwater and I couldn't make out what she was saying. I turned away from her and began to swim, towards the other side of the ditch, but there was someone crouching in the foliage. It was the Killer, the face from the newspaper, not human but as he looked in the artist's impression, a two-dimensional, black and white mesh of pencil strokes. He waved and beckoned me towards him, dropping on all fours as he held out a paper arm for me to grab onto. I looked around wildly, treading the thick liquid and struggling not to sink. The world began to echo with the sound of Mum and Nan, as they shouted old ghost stories out to each other. Dick Roberts appeared, hanging blue from a tree, swinging to and fro on a noose and ticking like a pendulum. I covered my ears to make the noise stop and watched as his body splintered into a thousand cornflower petals. They rained down onto me, showering my face with soft, dead skin.

I woke up with a short shout and sprang up in bed, feeling tiny diamonds of hot sweat across my face. I was only half awake, I think, as I threw back the sticky bed sheets and automatically swung off the edge of the bunk, peering through the darkness to James's bed. But it was empty, of course. It seemed more so by the dim sight of it, freshly made and neatly tucked. It looked purposeless, ownerless: almost as if it had been caught in between breathing in and out, and was missing the protracted bump of a belly where James should have been.

The curtains curved black against the window sill. Objects lay scattered, distinctive only because of their familiar shapes. The teak drawers, cluttered with toys: a khakied Action Man, abandoned on his side; two Barbies, entwined where James had discarded them. They were naked. He had told me they were getting a bit of lesbian action.

He would have run away with the fair, just like he said.

He was all right, I told myself.

I was sure of it. Almost sure of it.

He had left ours and, in the spirit of

adventure, made his way to the most exotic person's caravan – the fortune-teller's, probably. And everyone knew that fortune-tellers were elderly, single women who had all wanted children but never got the chance.

He had said, hadn't he, that he was going to run away with the fair?

So that was where he'd be. In a fortune-teller's cabin, ensconced in the homely dis-array: all wooden screens and scruffy velvet, bright scarves hanging from doorways and red lighting. 'Rosie Lee', large painted letters would declare at the entrance of the caravan. 'Fortunes told'.

I stared up at the white swirls on the ceiling, and it was only then that I became properly aware of the noises drifting in from Mum's room next door.

The springs on the double bed were creak-ing – not in singular rhythmic concentration, like they sometimes did late at night when we were supposed to be asleep, but in a noisy, squeaky chaos – as she wheezed and heaved.

'Come on, bring it all up.' I heard Nan's voice, gruff yet soothing.

Mum spluttered in response.

After a while Nan's feet padded out from the bedroom and walked over the landing, to the toilet. She flushed something away and walked downstairs, calling, 'Give me a second, Katie. I'll be back in a minute.'

She stopped at the foot of the stairs – and the door to the living room – and said something to Dick Roberts that was drowned out by a fresh attack of splutters, from Mum's room. There came the rumble of Dick Roberts's reply, and then more. Next door was quiet again, and this time I could hear what Nan was saying.

'It's more than worry, Dick. She's bringing up blood, for God's sake. It's been going on for more than two weeks now. I'm sorry, I know it's your night off, but we're going to have to call the doctor.'

18

Nan B had tried to keep to her threat, and for two weeks after the trip to Leigh-on-Sea we didn't see her. It was only after a fortnight that she reappeared, albeit grudgingly, since Mum hadn't backed down or gone round to hers with a bouquet of apologies and tales of disaster.

'I could have been lying dead in my flat for the past couple of weeks, for all you cared,' she grumbled, huffily, but Mum wasn't in the mood for arguments.

'If you've come to cause trouble you can bugger off home,' she snapped in return. She could be surprisingly assertive sometimes. There were rare occasions when her maternal biology flashed out, and at those times Nan knew better than to cross her.

But it wasn't like Nan to back down without a fight, and although she held her peace that day it wasn't the end of the matter, not by far. She was only biding her time and as it went on, and the Roberts began to visit us in Oxford more and more, she entered into a lengthy campaign to turn Mum against them.

At first she tried her hand at making Mum feel guilty.

For instance, there was the whole thing with Mum's hair.

'What's happened to your hair?' Nan asked Mum one afternoon, when the Robertses were up for a visit but had disappeared for a stroll around the tatty sports field, which they seemed to like.

It was unusual to hear Nan speak at that point in time. At first she had stayed away during their visits, but then she'd changed her mind and had taken to coming over and positioning herself in her usual chair at the kitchen table. There was no reconciliation in the gesture: she only did it to numb the atmosphere with disapproving silence. The Cadaver in the Corner, Aunty Net called her. She didn't actually want to talk, just to make sure that no one else did. She succeeded. After a few thwarted attempts, Nan and Grampy R knew better to approach her, and acknowledged her presence – and authority – with nervous smiles and subdued conversations. 'Honestly,' I overheard Nan R complaining one night, 'it's like we've farted in church.'

It was probably for that reason that Mum flinched at the sound of Nan's voice, and nervously fingered her freshly highlighted curls.

'Do you like them?' she blushed, stammering slightly. 'Mum R thought it would look nice.'

Nan's face crumpled into a frown but she quickly recovered her composure, and smiled icily.

'Oh, it's Mum R now, is it?' she said, carefully enunciating each word. 'And I suppose that I'll be Margaret next?'

Mum's face fell.

'Oh, Mum,' she muttered, helplessly, her shoulders sagging.

It didn't work though. True, Nan's snide comments had an insidious, discomfiting effect, but they weren't catastrophic. The world didn't cave in, the situation didn't change, and the Robertses continued their visits, appearing almost every month with their battered suitcase, for a weeklong stay.

Dick Roberts's parents weren't the only visitors, either.

There were others, too. Along with Grampy and Nan R, brothers and sisters started to crawl out of the woodwork. There was Aunty Moira the Lesbian, Uncle Rob the Junky, and Aunty Deborah the Schizo. That's what Nan called them, at least. Uncle Rob rode a big motorbike and had black bruises all the way down his arms, just like us, along with navy tattoos saying 'Sharon' and 'Liz'. He'd rode all the way to Germany once, for a beer festival. Aunty Moira had spiky platinum hair and was with another woman when she came. Aunty Debbie appeared and stayed for three weeks. Sometimes she lay in bed all day, and other times she would come down and sweep us off our feet, carry us off to the local playground – the one nearest our house, this side of the field and opposite my school – and run around the dilapidated slides and swings and splintered wooden roundabout, joining in with the other children as they hopscotched over dog muck and negotiated broken glass.

'How can you let her?' Nan B asked accusingly, when Debbie was almost out of earshot. 'What if she flips out when she's with them? The next time you see them you'll be fishing them out murdered from some bushes in the park.'

'Mum!'

'You mark my words – she forgets her medication and that's it, they've had it.'

Nan made a slitting motion, baring her teeth and slicing her hand viciously across her throat.

She won that one, it has to be said. After that particular comment Mum didn't let us out with Aunty Debbie again.

It went on and on, through the weeks, in much the same vein. Nan would bowl an accusation over at Mum, and Mum would resignedly bat it away.

'Ruining my reputation,' Nan'd start, putting on her most reproachful face as she settled back into her chair and launched into a fresh offensive. 'I don't know, I never thought it would be you, Katie. You were always such a good girl.'

'Don't go on,' Mum would reply, rolling her eyes, ploughing on with the ironing or whatever she was doing, blowing her hair from her face as she stooped over the board. 'They're not so bad.'

'Not so bad? Listen to yourself. They've made you lose your morals as well.'

'Don't go on, I said.'

'Well, look at them all, bloody scavengers, swanning in and eating you out of house and home. They've all got different fathers, you told me before.'

'You'd like his mum if you'd give her half a chance.'

Nan snorted contemptuously.

'I'd sooner remarry my ex-husband,' she said, looking down her nose, and the scorn on her face was real.

Grampy R liked to meet us at the school gates when he was up visiting. You could see him waiting for us as we walked through the main door in an old tweed suit and trilby hat, standing stiffly, like an ancient tree in a flood, while the navy-blue current of uniformed children flowed noisily around

157

him. He always wore that suit, and I never saw him without the trilby when he was outside. His eyes peered from beneath it as he strained to distinguish us from the crowd, and his pink lips stood out from his grey face like a bright daub of paint, wavering on the cusp of a smile that would only fully emerge when he spotted us.

Then he'd wave shyly, and pluck Black Jacks and paper bags full of Flying Saucers from invisible places as we drew near.

He told us lots of different stories on the way home, that the rotten tree stumps in our school playground were the homes of fairies, who slept in the day and flew out and played at night, in the starry sky; that the green mound beside them was the stomach of a sleeping giant, who would one day wake and rise from his sleep, yawning loudly and shaking off the dirt and daisies with his stretching fists.

One day James was at football practice, and it was just Grampy and me. We took a roundabout way home, and meandered along the back streets of the estate rather than walking down the straight line of Cumberland Road. Grampy looked everywhere as he walked, taking in the rows of brick houses, the net curtains, the neat hedges in some gardens and the jungle of weeds in others. He rolled the street signs off the tip of his tongue – Field Avenue, Crowberry Path, Bullrush Place – pausing to tell me that the names were taken from the days before this was an estate, when it was a wood, an old greenwood, and farming fields that had hedgerows full of berries and flowers and birds.

'How do you know?'

'Because your mum told me. This estate was only built thirty, forty years ago. Before that it was countryside.'

'See,' he said, stopping when we got to Hazelnut Path, the little square behind our house, pointing at a lone tree, which had broken out into frail pink blossoms, 'that tree, I'll bet you a pound it was there when this whole place was covered with them. Now it's one of the only ones left.'

I clutched his hand and peered over at it, brushing my hair out of my face as I took in its knotty joints and the ravaged litter drifting aimlessly around it. It was a clear day, the type when the summer breaks for an afternoon through the drizzly spring, and the petals looked pretty against the blue sky.

'Look around,' Grampy whispered in my ear, struggling slightly as he bent down beside me. I heard his knee joints pop.

'What can you see?'

I looked but there wasn't much to see, really. Just houses on every side of me, monotonous brown rows with the same garden walls and the same thin windows. The exteriors differed slightly – some were tidy while others were scruffy and unkempt, some windows were clean while others were dirty – but underneath they were all the same. The maisonettes where Nan B lived stood to my right, decrepit with broken stairs and graffiti-tattoos. I could just about see our back bedroom window, which looked out onto them, over the garage roofs.

I shrugged. 'Nothing,' I said. 'Just houses.'

Grampy let out a pointed gasp. 'Nothing?' he said. 'Look harder.'

I looked again. A blue plastic bag fluttered softly, scraping the concrete and bobbing up into the air, drifting with the breeze. Round patches of chewing gum stained the grey pathway and crops of dandelions sprouted on the tuft of grass. A crushed biro wept blue ink into the dirt beside my feet as a boy from school swung open a gate and disappeared through a door. I turned around, and saw Amber Jenkins hovering in an alleyway to the side, covertly smoking a fag with a friend. She had her back to me, and her long dark hair fell over her new upper school uniform. She turned and caught me watching her, and scowled indifferently before turning away again.

An invisible bird chirruped.

Litter blanketed the ground.

If you looked hard enough through some of the windows you could just make out the outline of women standing at the kitchen sink, like Mum, doing the washing-up while keeping an eye on the road outside and their neighbours' houses, opposite.

'Nothing much,' I eventually repeated, shrugging again.

'Can't you see the gypsies?'

'No.'

Grampy frowned and said I would have to look harder. He could see them.

'I can't.'

'Well,' he said, picking himself up from his crouching position and stiffly brushing his tweed trousers down, 'you'll have to learn, then.'

There was another world, he told me, on top of ours, a magical one. It was invisible to most people but I might one day be able to see it, and if I did I'd find the Gypsies of Hazelnut Path. If I managed it, the scruffy houses would disappear together with the everyday people and instead I'd see the gypsy compound. There were old wooden caravans instead of houses, and one-eyed, gold-hooped women who read palms, and dark-haired fiddlers who played beautiful music, long into the night.

'When you're next round there,' he told me, as we continued walking and neared our front door, 'keep an eye on the blossom tree, because that tree is in their world as well.'

Look at it hard enough and for long enough, he said, and slowly this world will drift away and the gypsy world will get clearer and clearer.

'I'll be able to see it, one day?'

'Maybe, but only if you really want to and you try hard enough.'

He winked at me, his eyes sparkling, and ruffled my hair before we opened the door.

Mum was in the kitchen, looking flustered, when we entered.

'Can I have a packet of crisps?' I asked, but she ignored me.

Her purse was open on the side, and a few coppers were scattered on the vinyl around it.

'Anything wrong?' Grampy asked her, concerned.

Mum looked up at him, frowning.

'Oh nothing,' she said, mumbling as she looked back down at the money. 'Food money's gone and disappeared, that's all.'

She hesitated and glanced out of the window.

'Dick must have taken it without telling me,' she said, in the end.

Grampy looked over at Nan R, who was sitting by the table. They raised their eyebrows at each other and Grampy turned back towards Mum, dipping his hands in his jacket pocket.

'We can always give–' he began, bringing out his wallet, but Mum, seeing what he was about to do, blushed and cut him off.

'Don't be silly,' she said hastily, waving him away. 'I've got some money upstairs, I can always dip into that.'

'You sure?'

'Yeah – yes.'

She leaned back against the sideboard, as Grampy tucked the wallet back in his pocket, and rubbed one hand tiredly across her eyes.

'He must have forgotten to tell me, that's all,' she said, smiling limply, but she didn't disguise the worry in her voice.

19

On Thursday I stayed at Aunty Net's while Mum went up the hospital with Nan. I didn't know why they were going. I just knew that they'd spent the morning up the doctor's, and that when they arrived back they told Dick Roberts that they had to go up to the John Radcliffe, way up in Headington, and if he looked after the house and waited for any news, they'd take me over to Net's.

Aunty Net was in the dark, as well.

'Mind your own,' Nan had said when she asked her what was going on. 'It would make a bloody change.'

Aunty Net scowled and stood watching them from behind the net curtains, as they sat at the bus stop across the road.

'Mind your own,' she mimicked irritably, scrunching up her face. 'Mind your own, for a bloody change.'

She waited until Nan and Mum had climbed onto the bus and then hurried over to her handbag. She emptied the contents, scattering rusting coins, rumpled tissues, a couple of old screw-top bottle-tops and a DHSS booklet over the floor, until she found what she was after: an old, scuffed leather purse, from which she plucked a battered five-pound note.

'There we are,' she said, holding it in the air as she smiled at me pleadingly with orange teeth. 'Pop up the shops for me, would you, ducky?'

I reluctantly took the money and looked down at the queen's face.

'I'm not allowed to go out by myself,' I complained, but she brushed my protests aside, pushing me out of the living room and towards the front door.

'Go on, luvvie, I'm half parched, I tell you, I've not had a drop since your brother did a runner.'

I knew that wasn't the truth; she smelled a bit funny already. I left the house anyway, wondering as I walked where she had been getting her medicine from without James or me to help her.

When I got back I pushed some clothes, dirty plates and old milk cartons off from the sofa and onto the floor, taking a seat. A trickle of lumpy liquid dribbled out of a carton and onto the carpet, but it didn't really matter. The house was so generally squalid that another mucky puddle wasn't going to hurt. I watched as Manilow prowled around the room. He paused briefly at the white trail, sniffing it curiously, before moving on and settling for a piece of old, indistinguishable food on a plate in a corner. He probably ate more than Aunty Net, I thought, although like Aunty Net his eyes oozed and scaled with sticky grunge and his tabby fur – like her hair – was falling out in greasy clumps.

Aunty Net sat in the middle of the living-room floor, her own eyes glowing as she unscrewed the bottle. Her legs were tucked beneath her coiled body: she sat, poised like an aged nymph, surrounded by the dirty fibre flowers of the ancient, patterned carpet.

She must have been pretty, once. You could see it shining out from old photos. There was a kind of ravaged beauty about her, even now, at least when she was animated.

'You must miss that little brother of yours, pet,' she mumbled, but her thoughts were really elsewhere. She scrabbled around until she found an old, cloudy glass, holding it up before her as though it were a diamond-encrusted genie's lamp, filling it right up, to the very brim with the clear

166

liquid from the bottle.

'Cheers,' she giggled, holding the glass high in the air and downing the contents in one go.

She belched, and wiped the spit from her mouth with the back of her hand.

'Mind your own,' she repeated sadly, and let out a loud sigh.

Then she filled up the bottle cap with the liquid, and knelt down with her elbows on the ground, holding it out to the cat.

'Manny? Meow? Come and have a drink with your mummy!' she cooed.

Manilow carried on eating from the plate, ignoring her.

She turned and held the cap towards me.

'Want it?' she asked. When I quickly shook my head, she shrugged, and swallowed the measure herself.

'I don't know,' she grumbled. 'Bloody swotty kids. I was smoking when I was eight.'

She sat silently after that and her eyes swerved purposelessly around the living room until they came to rest on me again. I squirmed uncomfortably, and tried to avoid the intensity of her gaze, focusing on the television, where *Why Don't You?* was on.

'I'll tell you something, though,' Aunty Net said. 'If anyone knows where your brother is, it's you. Isn't that right, little miss?'

I didn't know how to react and sat, trying to wipe the surprise off my face, as I mutely shook my head. It was just like her, to come out with something like that.

'Look at you, sitting there as if butter wouldn't melt in your mouth.'

She let out a sharp cackle and, reaching out over the floor, patted my head.

'Don't you worry, my little darling,' she said. 'As long as you're sure he's all right, your secret's safe with me.'

Aunty Net got livelier and livelier. She alternated between lying on the floor and performing a strange whirling dance around the living room. The now empty bottle was her partner; she held it tightly to her chest as though it were a fragile and precious child. Eventually she collapsed back onto the carpet, her ragged skirt splayed around her and began, hiccupingly, to tell me of the Roman soldier a friend of a friend had seen, walking through the park the other day.

'And it occurred to me, didn't it? Didn't it?' she shouted excitedly, wagging her fist in the air. 'I tell you, it suddenly hit me that there used to be an old Roman road around here, and that was why she could only see half his body, because that old road is buried under our one. It's lower down, eh?'

I nodded.

'You see?' she shouted.

She tried to get to her feet but failed, falling back onto the ground.

'I'll get you a cup of tea, Aunty Net.'

She lifted her face from the carpet and pouted at me.

'It will make you feel better,' I hazarded.

Her features continued to darken.

'Listen to yourself. Tea? *"Cup of tea, Aunty Net?"* Chip off the old block, you. Bloody Bainbridge through and through.'

'It might make you feel better–'

'Oh, listen to it,' she spat at an invisible audience. *"It might make you feel better. Cup of tea, Aunty Net? One single cup of tea and you'll never need your medicine again."*

She picked up a rusting knitting needle that lay by her side and threw it limply across the room at me.

'Just like your mother,' she snapped, 'but all the tea in China's not changed her rotten luck.'

Her coiled body swayed, and then lurched sideways. She toppled down onto the ground and her head landed with a painful thud on the carpet. It didn't seem to bother

her though. She didn't move again, and after a few silent minutes she began to softly snore.

'Aunty Net?'

I whispered softly in her ear and tugged half-heartedly at her naked, carpet-creased arm. It thumped flaccidly to the ground again as soon as I let go. Her breaths were long and heavy.

'Aunty Net!'

There was no use. A green string of saliva hung from her mouth, trickling down and soaking into the threadbare carpet. Her eyes rolled half open, half closed.

My tummy rumbled.

'Aunty Net?' I said, trying one last time and placing a tentative hand on her shoulder.

At last she stirred, but it was only to bat me away.

'Leave me be,' she managed to groan, before she fell back into sleep.

Despondent, I gave up and wandered into the kitchen, skidding over some oil on the lino as I walked through the door.

It seemed impossible that Aunty Net's kitchen – her whole house, in fact – and ours had an identical layout. They managed to look so different. She had the same kitchen units as us, the ones that had come with the house, but whereas Mum bleached and sprayed and scrubbed ours all day long, Aunty Net just left hers to nature. The surfaces were cracked and peeling, tiles hung off from the ceiling and the floor stuck to your socks. Half-eaten food lay everywhere – on the floor, on the tables – piles of it, rotting like an abandoned wedding feast.

She really didn't care, Aunty Net, but there was a gentleness in the neglect. She didn't subdue anything; she simply let things grow around her.

I pulled open one of the rickety cupboard doors, and rifled through sticky packages in the hope of discovering something I could eat. A Nescafé jar lay on its side, the last few grains of coffee dissolving on the plastic; a Yorkshire pudding mix, gnawed open by mice, spewed flour over a couple of tins of Nisa baked beans. I picked one up, but any hope of cooking it dissolved when I turned and took a look at the cooker. In the end, in amongst the multitude of empty bottles and some plastic packets of powdered mash potato, I found some out-of-date jelly babies.

I popped them into my skirt pocket and walked over to the sink, looking for a cloth to mop up the oil, when Nan let herself in.

'Where's Net?' she asked, standing in the kitchen as she took off her scarf.

She wasn't looking at me and didn't seem to need an answer. Her eyes fluttered briefly over the room, taking in the cobwebs and the grease stains sliding up the walls.

'Christ, look at the state of this place,' she said, loudly, wrinkling her nose. 'And what's that smell?'

She walked over to the bin, flipped open the lid – muttering something about Mum and the worry as she did – and lurched hurriedly away when she saw what was in it. She sighed, rolling her eyes.

'Just nipping to the loo,' she said.

She didn't stop to look in the living room before she disappeared upstairs into the toilet.

I held my breath and listened to her footsteps up the stairs, waiting until I heard the toilet door close before hurrying in to Aunty Net. She'd be in trouble if Nan found her asleep on the floor. I'd probably be in trouble too.

'Aunty Net, wake up!' I whispered urgently.

I tapped her shoulder but she lay silent and prostrate, aside from the strange gurgling sound that bubbled up from her lips.

'Aunty Net! *Aunty Net!*'

The toilet chain flushed.

The toilet door creaked open.

Panicking, I grabbed her dandruffed curls and wrenched her head up into the air. She jerked, and began to rattle and choke. I could hear Nan's footsteps on the stairs. Oh God, I thought, we're in for it – but then Aunty Net came to with a violent start and shook herself awake. She heaved herself up onto all fours, crouching like a down-trodden, stray dog as she retched into the already sodden ground. Her cheeks were sweaty with bile and flecked with tiny grains of dirt. One half of her hair stood up on end.

I stood watching her, unsure of what I should do.

'Nan's here,' I whispered, helplessly, grabbing her arm and trying to pull her towards the sofa.

But it was too late. Nan was already at the living-room door. She stood, her headscarf in her hand, watching Aunty Net as she writhed pathetically, on all fours, on the floor.

'What the hell is going on here?' she asked quietly, her eyes thin slits, her lips pursed.

20

'I don't know, just try to keep calm. Don't go saying anything silly.'

Mum was talking to Aunty Net. Their heads were bowed and inclined slightly towards each other as they stood at the kitchen sink. Mum was peeling potatoes with a paring knife and passing them on to Aunty Net, who chopped them into chips with another knife on the draining board, and then dropped the thick rectangles into a bowl of cold water by her side.

Aunty Net looked different the year Nan and Grampy R were visiting. She'd stopped drinking for a while round then. She and Mum were discussing the meeting that was to take place the following day. It was with the Social Services, deciding access rights. It was going to take place at the children's home, and it would be the first time that Aunty Net had seen her kids for six months. Valerie and Jason. I liked them, but they were too old for us – there was five years' difference, and more, between us.

'Just tell them the truth,' Mum was saying. She plunged a half-peeled potato into the washing-up bowl, wiping the dirt off with the tepid water and holding the potato briefly up to the light before she dunked it again and carried on peeling. 'Just tell them that Pete's gone, you're off the drink and you miss your kids, that's all you need to say.'

Mum was an inch or two taller than Aunty Net, but that was about the only difference. Neither of them were tall. With their backs to us, facing the window, they looked practically the same, with their short black curls and pastel T-shirts, and the synchrony of chopping and peeling.

From the front, Aunty Net looked younger than usual. Her eyes were clear, and apart from the psoriasis the blotchiness of her skin had all but disappeared. But her movements seemed clumsier, denser somehow, as though she were waking from sleep and gathering her bearings. Her conversation was like that too. She wasn't the cocksure Aunty Net that we knew, at least not as much as she normally was. She frequently appeared round at ours, asking Mum for a cup of tea and her opinion.

'What if they don't believe me, what if the kids don't want to come home?'

'Bit late to be getting worried now,' Mum replied. Her voice was even and measured, in contrast to the nervous edge in Aunty Net's. 'Just don't lose your temper, that's all.'

She shook a potato, the drops flying through the air like a wet dog shaking its coat, and then passed it along.

'That enough?' she asked, craning her neck to take a look at the chips.

'One more,' Aunty Net said. 'That should be enough then, I'd have thought.'

She sighed heavily, and paused for a minute before she spoke. It sounded like it cost her to change the subject.

'Where's Her Highness got to, anyway?' she asked.

'Christ knows. Sticking pins in Voodoo dolls, I should think.'

They laughed softly together, the mood briefly lightened, and then it was Mum's turn to hesitate before she spoke.

'Don't tell her this,' she said, speaking slowly, choosing her words, 'but some bits and bobs have been going missing from the house.'

Aunty Net stopped chopping and glanced over at her sister.

'What do you mean?'

Mum shrugged. 'A bit of money here and

there, that's all – nothing much, but it's hard enough to get by as it is.'

Aunty Net half opened her mouth to say something more, but stopped when she saw Grampy and Nan R opening the garden gate. They'd gone up the shops for Mum, to get her another pack of eggs to go with the chips, and they entered the kitchen, plucking off their coats and shaking the rain from them.

'There we go,' Nan R shouted, passing the eggs over to Mum and rummaging in her wallet for the change.

She handed it over, and then sat down heavily on one of the kitchen chairs, taking off her glasses and rubbing them with her cardigan sleeve.

'Ernie, go and get my eye-drops, will you? They're stinging a bit,' she rumbled, squinting up at him before she turned her attention back to the thick lenses.

Preoccupied, she didn't notice the glance that Aunty Net and Mum exchanged before they turned back towards the sink.

'She should be here any minute,' Mum said, looking up at the clock as she impatiently strummed the worktop with her fingers.

Dick Roberts was back, watching television

in the living room, and Mum, Aunty Net, Nan and Grampy R sat in the kitchen, drinking mugs of tea while they waited for Nan B to arrive. Mum leaned against the kitchen units, while the other three sat around the table.

'Can't we eat without her?' Aunty Net asked, after another five minutes had passed, but Mum only raised her eyebrows and shook her head.

'It'd only be one more nail in the coffin if we do,' she said, shortly.

Aunty Net rolled her eyes. 'Silly old cow,' she said. 'It's her own bloody fault for being so late.'

When Mum didn't answer she looked to the Robertses, scrutinizing them for some show of assent. Grampy R blushed, and averted his eyes.

Aunty Net saw his face and laughed. She liked Grampy R.

'You can't fool me, Ern,' she teased. 'You must think she's a silly old cow too, the way she's been treating you.'

But Grampy R only shuffled uncomfortably in his seat, and lowered his eyes to the floor.

'She's probably got her reasons,' he mumbled.

'Oh yeah, she's got her reasons, green-eyed monster reasons, amongst other things–' Aunty Net began, but stopped when she saw the expression on Mum's face.

She paused, taking a sip of tea, then she said: 'You'd never think that it was her that introduced Katie and Dick in the first place, would you, the way that she carries on.'

Nan R looked up. 'That right?' she said, smiling wryly.

'Yeah.' Aunty Net chattered on, happy to talk. She seemed a bit on edge that night, nervous, as if she wanted to keep talking in order to put something else to the back of her mind. 'Mum took in lodgers for a while, after she kicked the old man out – needed a bit of extra cash – and Dick stayed with her when he first started up at The Works. Saw the advert in the shop window and turned up on the doorstep. She was living up in Cowley, then, up Holloway. Anyway, you were back at home, weren't you, Katie? I think Mum was getting a bit worried about her ending up on the shelf.'

'I was only twenty-four. You make it sound like I was an old maid!' Mum interrupted from across the room, but she was laughing.

'You bloody were, in those days,' Aunty Net said. 'Twenty-five and you were past it.

I was married when I was eighteen, or else I might have ended up marrying your son myself.'

'Net–'

'Eighteen, I was. Just a baby. Four months up the duff and damaged goods by the time Mum managed to drag me up the aisle. She went around to that poor old sod's house and stayed there till he agreed he'd marry me.'

'Net!'

'What?' She turned, glancing over at Mum and nudging Nan R conspiratorially. 'Look at her, blushing like she's the Virgin Mary. I sometimes wonder how she managed to have two kids. Turkey basting, was it, Katie?'

Mum blushed even more.

Aunty Net laughed. 'Lenny Godfrey, do you remember?' she mused. A smile, half wistful, flickered over her face. 'My first husband,' she explained to Nan R. 'Bloody swine, that one. Lazy bastard.'

'You do pick them,' Mum said, as she reached for her cigarettes.

Aunty Net snorted. 'Look who's bloody talking,' she started, but Mum had shot her another warning look. 'Anyway, where was I? So, yeah: Mum's just got Katie left to worry about — and she's really starting to worry, by this stage, you know, that she's going to have her eldest daughter living off her welfare cheque till Kingdom Come. She must have thought her prayers were answered when Prince Charming came knocking at the door.'

Nan R laughed. 'I don't know if I'd go as far as Prince Charming,' she said.

Aunty Net nodded, agreeing with her as she stooped over, lighting up a cigarette. She took a deep drag, making the amber of the cigarette flare one, two, three times, and then sat back again, blowing a series of smoke rings into the air.

'You don't need to tell me,' she said, 'but that was how she saw him, honestly. You'd never think it, but there was a time when our mum thought the sun shone out of that man's arse.

The doorbell rang.

Mum jumped.

'Shh! She hears you laughing and there'll be sour grapes all evening,' she hissed, hastily disappearing to open the front door.

But if there was one thing that could be said for Nan B, it was that she was governed by her own rules.

She wore her pink chiffon scarf again that

night and breezed cheerfully into the kitchen, impervious to the stunned silence as she delicately peeled the fragile square from her white curls and smiled brightly over at the nonplussed people clustered at the kitchen table.

'Sorry I'm late,' she said, talking directly to Nan and Grampy R. 'Got caught up with something.'

She'd never addressed them before. Not once.

She paused in the middle of the room, blinking through her glasses and examining faces as she took off her coat and waited pointedly for a response, but the shock of hearing her was so great that no one, at first, could quite manage a reply.

'Hope I haven't kept you waiting,' she prompted.

But no one knew how to react.

Grampy R flinched ever so slightly, rearing away from the sudden volte-face. I sympathized with him. For months now, Nan B had spoken to us only in frigid tones.

Nan R shifted awkwardly in her chair, which creaked disobligingly beneath her as she struggled to straighten her mammoth frame. After some effort she managed to uncross her legs and sat, like an uneasy schoolgirl in a headmistress's office, with her hands folded self-consciously in her lap. Her thick lips had lolled open in an 0 of mute surprise before she hastily realigned her mouth into a nervous, appeasing smile.

Even Aunty Net was momentarily taken aback. Her eyebrows shot up into her hair and her eyes flicked over to Mum before she regained her composure and relaxed back into her seat, taking another long drag of the cigarette that had been suspended mid-air. For a second or two she looked like her old self as the ghost of a smirk flitted across her face.

But Nan B didn't seem to notice.

It was as though the months of unilateral antagonism had never happened.

'Want a hand, Katie?' she asked, un-abashed, putting her coat and bag down on the side.

Mum had scurried into the kitchen after Nan, blinking wildly for a moment or two as though clearing any impediment to her vision and making sure that the change in Nan's posture was not simply a component of a surreal dream. ('She kissed my cheek when I opened the door,' she told Aunty Net, later. 'I had to pinch myself.')

But she knew better than to rock the boat.

'Could you set the table?' was all she said, trying her hardest to look nonchalant as she turned to flick the switch of the deep fat fryer and then picked up Nan B's things and took them to hang up. As she turned towards us, I caught the bright, surprised moons of her eyes.

Nan nodded willingly and her fingers briefly reached out and brushed Mum's shoulder as she stretched up to pluck dinner plates from the overhead cupboard.

Aunty Net sat watching them with veiled eyes, blowing out long, serpentine ribbons of smoke.

'Parting of the Red Sea's next on the programme, I expect,' I heard her mumble beneath her breath.

21

Dick Roberts looked tired – exhausted, even. There were navy bags beneath his eyes, his thin lips sloped in an ugly downward curve and his hair seemed more salt than pepper. He walked into the kitchen and slung his holdall down to the floor, trailing his dirty fingers over his forehead and into his hair, shooting a reluctant nod at Nan and glaring over at me before he turned to the newspaper, which was lying on the side.

'Don't just sit there,' he snapped, casting his eyes around the room. 'Get off your backside and put the milk bottles out.'

Nan stood at the other side of the unit by the cooker, with her back to him, chopping her way through a bowl of carrots. She didn't look round when he spoke.

'Leave them there,' she said. 'There's no hurry.'

Dick Roberts's lips tightened, but he didn't argue.

'No news?' he grunted, as he flicked warily through the pages of the *Oxford Mail*.

Nan shook her head in reply but Dick Roberts, with his back turned, didn't see. He must have thought she was ignoring him, and his temper flared.

'No news, I said.'

'No,' Nan spat. She stopped what she was doing and turned to face him, slapping her knife onto the chopping board. Folding her arms, she looked him up and down through thin, angry slits. 'No. The police are coming round tomorrow. They're talking about doing a proper search of some kind, if he's not back by then. I don't expect he will be. If I were your son, I think I'd prefer to keep myself hidden.'

'What do you mean, proper search?'

'I didn't realize there was more than one meaning.'

'How's she taken it?'

'Who's "she"? The cat's mother?'

'You know who I mean.'

But Nan only raised her eyebrows and primly pursed her lips before turning back to the vegetables.

'She's gone half crazy with worry, if that's what you're asking,' she said. 'But at least her bruises are fading.'

'Stop chamming.'

It was just Nan, Dick Roberts and me for tea. Aunty Net would have been coming round but Nan had banned her from the house after yesterday.

'Pull yourself together, my girl, and you might get a bit of sympathy,' she scolded, when Aunty Net accused her of cruelty.

Tea was a casserole. Sausages with carrots and potatoes. Nan had made it from scratch, no packets or nothing. That was one of the best things about Mum being in bed and Nan staying, because everything Mum ever cooked came out of a packet. The only thing she could manage was chips. She trusted the germ-busting strength of the deep fat fryer, knew it wouldn't let her down. As for the rest, a horror of e-coli and salmonella made her overzealous in her food preparations; vegetables were stewed in seismic water for three-quarters of an hour, and Sunday roasts emerged from the oven like the charred remains of an unsuccessful crematorium fire.

After serving up our portions, Nan put hers in the oven and one more plateful of it onto a red plastic tray, which she carried upstairs, to Mum's room.

The gentle murmur of their voices drifted downstairs.

Dick Roberts and I were left alone.

'I said stop chamming. And get your elbows off the table.'

He jabbed a finger into my shoulder and sneered menacingly before picking up his knife and fork once more.

'You'll be seeing the back of my hand in a minute,' he muttered, as a potato disappeared into his mouth.

We carried on eating.

I tried to chew very quietly.

He was spoiling for a fight, but Dick

Roberts seemed restless as well as bad-tempered. He ate a mouthful of food and then put down his cutlery, craning his neck to look out of the dip in the curtains or throwing a warning glare at me. He kept sighing, his shoulders sagged, and a couple of times he wiped his palm tiredly across clenched eyes. His hands were black with oil and left a long, greasy smear over his eyebrow.

He hadn't bothered to change and was still in his overalls. They were splattered with silver paint and smelled arid and sweaty, as if they were permeated with hard work.

'I. Said. Get. Your. Elbows. Off. The. Table.'

He irritably swung over and pushed my arm. My elbow tripped and the fork jogged towards me and before I could stop it the piece of speared sausage flew off the prongs and through the air, sending brown drops flying over the table and Dick Roberts's plate, before it dropped limply onto my skirt. I picked it up with my fingers, but it was hot and sloppy from the gravy.

'Ouch,' I said, dropping it quickly and blowing my fingers.

It plopped onto the floor.

I looked down at it.

I didn't have to look at him. I knew I was

in for it.

I took an unsteady breath as he lurched towards me, kicking his chair back and scattering the dinner things out over the table, and waited for the first blow.

It came, a hard slam on my right cheek. The force of it knocked my head around.

Time seemed to both slow down and speed up then. Definitions intensified and distorted until – as each thump descended – I was left with the evening sun pouring through the window and the neat stacks of washing-up beside the kitchen sink. I could make out every detail: the indents of the brown stripes against the white enamel of the saucepans, the strands of scum hanging down like cobwebs from their rims.

The silvery scratches on an aluminium colander twinkled with an odd, sunset aura.

'What does it take to teach you some manners?' Dick Roberts shouted as he switched from my head and started smacking ferociously at my legs.

A few tears sprinkled over my bare arms.

My ears started to fill with a strange thumping hum.

Then it happened.

He had just started having a go at my head again, yanking my hair into a tight ponytail as he slapped – right and left, right and left – when suddenly Mum, who had been so quiet and still since Wednesday, hardly speaking at all, even giving up on phoning the police station, burst through the kitchen door.

She looked wild; her short black curls stuck out from her head like a stormy aura and her teeth, her snarling mouth, seemed almost feral. She grabbed the nearest thing to her, which was a milk bottle, and smashed it down on the counter.

He let go of my hair.

The crystalline fragments sprayed out all over the room, scattering with a tinkle, and she jabbed the jagged stump at Dick Roberts's face.

'*I'll fucking kill you,*' she screamed.

But it was over as soon as it started. Her voice was shaky with fear; the anger spent. She leaned against the side, winded, catching her breath. Her contorted face collapsed back into its usual frame and she looked, once more, like a frail, beaten woman. The yellowing bruises seemed to whirl and clash, like autumn clouds, over her quivering face.

'Come on, love, come on,' Nan said gently, tugging her arm and trying to pry the bottle away from her hands. But she held on, and she continued to shake it vaguely in his direction, though most of her energy had disappeared.

'You ever touch my kids,' she said, 'you ever...'

But she was gasping by then, and crying, and her words came out in sobs. She dropped the bottle to the ground and Nan B put her arms around her.

'Come on, love.'

'This is your fault. *Your fault.* He ran away because of you and he's probably dead and the police couldn't care less and you – you touch my kids again – you ever...'

Dick Roberts took a shaky step forward, cutting through Mum's moans to brush his hand down her dressing-gown sleeve. Nan slapped his arm out of the way.

'Don't *you* touch her,' she snarled at him, turning her daughter gently around and leading her back through the kitchen door.

Watching their retreating figures made me want to cry more than being hit did. Maybe it was their heads bowed together, the one black, the one grey, their bodies so close that they seemed almost to be bleeding into each other. And the tender, reassuring noises that Nan was making.

Nan paused and swivelled her head around towards me, cocking her chin for me to follow.

'Come on, poppet,' she said, softly. 'Come upstairs, with us.'

Dick Roberts followed us to the bottom of the stairs.

'I'll go and have a look around the estate, shall I?' he asked.

His arms were hanging by his side, his body seemed to sag forward heavily, limp like a puppet with broken strings. I was too far up the stairs to make out the expression in his eyes.

Nobody bothered to reply.

22

Nan's new-found benevolence didn't have chance to last long, because the Robertses disappeared as suddenly and curiously as they had arrived.

Dick Roberts never mentioned them, not until the day he learned that Grampy R was dead. Nan only ever talked about them when he was away from the house.

Good for Nothings, she called them then, having reverted to her previous frame of mind. Better off without them, she said.

They had suddenly stopped visiting when Mum discovered some things missing from her bedroom.

A ring at first. Her engagement ring.

It happened on the day that she set aside for a spring-clean. Mum's spring-cleans weren't to be taken lightly. They were full-blown affairs, a zealous war against filth, with buckets and mops, J-cloths, scourers, rubber gloves and a mystifying heap of liquids and sprays: Mr Sheen for the furniture, Ajax for the bathroom, Windolene for the glass. She wielded old-fashioned feather dusters, jabbing them like rapiers at cobwebs in corners, even though there were never any cobwebs there.

She liked it though, however much she tried to hide behind her grumbling huffs and puffs. You could tell from the luminous expression on her face, which lit up like she was having a conversation with God. She dressed in her old clothes on those days, a pair of scuffed jeans and a paint-splattered shirt, and tied her hair up in an old tatty scarf.

'You look like a bloody Land Girl,' Nan

told her, but Mum only waved her aside, snapping that she had more important things to do than spend all day gassing about nothing.

On those days, Spring-Clean Days – which came about once every three months, with the seasons – the world was turned upside down.

Windows were cleaned, furniture was scrubbed, the contents of cutlery drawers were emptied into a sink filled with bleach, wardrobes of clothes were rearranged and picture frames were dusted.

Not even the jewellery box escaped a clean-out.

And that was when the trouble started.

The house, which had hummed with the noise of the hoover for the best part of the morning, was quiet. After lugging it back to the cupboard beneath the stairs, Mum had clapped her hands together, satisfied, and made herself a cup of tea and a cheese and Branston pickle sandwich. She'd eaten it standing up, leaning against the kitchen sink, before disappearing up to her bedroom.

'You don't have to hang around,' she said to Nan, before she left the kitchen. 'Go and check on Net or something.'

But Nan shook her head. 'I'm fine, I'm fine,' she said, her eyes on the paper in front of her. 'Got the crossword to finish, anyway.'

The day ticked by.

It was a rainy afternoon and we couldn't be bothered with going out and getting wet. James sat slouched at the table opposite Nan, with his chin cupped in his hands, reading a *Beano*. Occasionally he let out a melodramatically bored sigh, and tried to kick my head with his feet.

'Stop it!' I hissed, after the fifth time.

I checked to make sure that Nan wasn't looking, held up the compass I was using and jabbed it into his sock.

He screamed, grabbing his foot with his hand.

'*Nan!*'

She glared up from her paper. 'Will you be quiet!'

'I'm bleeding!'

But Nan wasn't looking at him any more. She was looking at Mum, who had come back down and was standing in the kitchen doorway.

'What's up, love?'

Mum didn't reply at first. She just stood, staring over at Nan.

'Love?'

'My engagement ring's missing, that's what.'

Nan B didn't respond straight away. She didn't look surprised, but then she hardly ever did. She watched Mum, scrutinizing her expression, then plucked out a B&H from the packet. After lighting up, she pulled herself out of her chair and stood, slowly brushing her pinafore down.

'Well,' she said, and she managed to sound level and business-like, even though her voice was muffled, what with the fag in her mouth. 'I s'pose we should go and check if anything else has gone.'

Mum nodded and they left the room.

We listened to their footsteps walking up the stairs overhead, and glanced at each other.

James turned back to his *Beano*.

'Do that again,' he mumbled, 'and I'll cut your hair off when you're asleep.'

Nan and Mum sat opposite each other at the kitchen table, quietly chain-smoking.

Mum gazed fixedly at the ground, and her expression was a kind of glazed shock.

'Our rainy day money,' she murmured, softly, shaking her head as though she couldn't quite believe what she was saying.

She took another long drag. Smoke curled up and met the higher drift of half a packet's worth of fog.

'After everything we've done for them,' she said.

She exchanged glances with Nan B, who gave a stoical sigh and raised her shoulders and palms up as though to say: What can you do?

'I – I was just going to ignore the other things,' Mum stammered, 'but this—'

'I did try to tell you, Katie,' Nan said, shaking her head. 'I did try, but – you know – I held my peace in the end and tried to give them the benefit of the doubt, for your sake.'

She tapped some ash into an ashtray.

Mum nodded. Her lips quivered.

'I know, Mum,' she said. 'I'm sorry.'

Nan smiled sadly, and reached out to pat Mum on the arm.

'Well, what's done is done,' she said.

She stood up and walked over to the kettle, filling it up with water and turning it on.

'Want a cup of tea?' she asked. 'Or something a bit stronger?'

'Tea.'

'You can't take any more risks though,' Nan said. She twitched the curtains, looking out onto the empty road before turning to Mum. 'You've got the kids to think about.'

Mum nodded again.

'No, I know,' she agreed, sighing heavily. Her mouth drooped. She lit up another cigarette.

Dick Roberts and Mum argued long and hard, that night. He kicked and spat and roared, but she stood her ground.

'Not in my house,' we heard her saying, despite all the banging and thumping.

'I'm not having it,' she said.

23

Violence wasn't in Mum's nature – even though she had to put up with it in the day to day – so it was no surprise that her burst of temper didn't last for long. The surge of emotion pushed her over the edge in another way, though. It was as if something inside her snapped: the week of worry and tension finally caught up with her and everything came tumbling out.

Nan managed to get her upstairs quietly enough. Mum whimpered softly, one arm flung over Nan's shoulders for support. But then when she got into the bedroom she collapsed, face down, on the bed, and started to sob. I watched her, hovering in the doorway, only vaguely registering as the front door opened and shut and Dick Roberts left the house.

'Katie,' Nan was saying, sitting on the edge of the bed.

She patted Mum's back, and used the same soft voice she had used downstairs.

'Come on, love. This is no good.'

Mum kneaded the pillows with her chewed, chapped hands. She was sprawled over the top covers, with her nightie hitched halfway up her blotchy legs, flashing her knickers and her saggy, psoriasis-marked thighs.

'I can't bear it! I can't bear it!' she spluttered, between sobs and coughs.

I got a glimpse of her face as she twisted it round, and saw a line of snot coming out from her nose. It was only then that it occurred to me her worst fear might be right. That he could be dead, after all.

'Katherine. Come on, I said,' Nan said.

'That's enough. Katie, come on. Come on. Enough, I said. Enough.'

Mum didn't listen.

Her cries got louder, her words more confused.

'Pull yourself together. You're frightening the poor kiddie.'

But Mum only howled, louder and louder. The noises she was making sounded as though they came from somewhere deep inside, as though they had been saved up for a long time. And in between, she uttered half-sentences, twisted and broken:

'Where is h–'

'My bab–'

'He's probably d–'

All the time shaking.

Reddening and reddening.

Until at last Nan wrenched Mum's arm, forcing her up, and – shouting, *'Katherine!'* at the top of her voice – slapped her once, hard, on her cheek. Mum slivered from the bed to her knees on the floor, knocking the gyrating Elvis clock, which fell with her and started to scream and scream.

'He's at the fair. He ran away with the fair,' I blurted.

Neither of them heard.

'I know where he is!'

'What?' Nan barely glanced round, just long enough for me to see wide, fazed eyes.

'Go to your bedroom,' she said as, crouching down, she took Mum's shoulders and started to shake her. 'Go on, love.'

'James is–'

'Go to your room!'

'But James...'

I went. The last thing I saw was Nan shaking Mum, trying to shout her into some kind of calm. I could hear her all the way to our bedroom, over Mum's cries: that James would be back soon and that the test results would be through in a few days and that this was all just a hiccup and did she want to end up like her sister and that she needed to calm down, calm down, for God's sake, because what good was getting all worked up – like this – going to do anyone? When I got back to my bedroom I wiped my face and crawled under the bottom bunk, to reach for the picture of the Killer, the artist's impression that had been in Wednesday's *Oxford Mail*. I'd cut it out and kept it.

It was still there.

I sat on the carpet, looking at him, trying to block out the noise.

His charcoal eyes stared up at me. Impassive, remote.

'Help us,' I whispered, smoothing the creases in the flimsy paper. 'Bring my brother back, if you can hear me. Please.'

24

'Well?' Nan asked, when she visited the next day.

But Mum only shrugged, looking sad.

'I just can't believe they did it, somehow,' she said.

Nan tutted disapprovingly, and raised her eyebrows as she pulled off her coat.

'Well, you'd be a fool to ignore what's right there in front of your own eyes,' she retorted. 'What are you going to do, let them come back and make you look like even more of an idiot?'

'No, course not.'

'That's my girl.'

Nan paused, looking at Mum for a second before she reached into her handbag and pulled out a thick envelope.

'Here,' she said, holding it out to Mum. 'Take it.'

'What is it?'

'Open it and see.'

Mum tore through the paper, and gasped when she pulled out a thick wad of notes. A couple of them slid through her fingers and drifted, swayingly, down to the carpet. She stood stunned for a while, in the middle of the kitchen, with the torn envelope and the money in her hands, looking from it, to Nan, then back again.

'I can't take this,' she said eventually, her voice choked.

She held the notes back out to Nan, who looked annoyed and waved them away.

'Don't be silly,' she snapped. 'I've been saving it all for an emergency like this.'

'But it must have taken years, this amount of money.'

They jostled for a while, yes-ing and no-ing, until in the end, to save an argument, Nan simply picked up her coat and walked out, leaving the money on the side.

'Just you remember,' she said before she left. 'You can always rely on true family.'

After Nan left, Mum lit up a cigarette and smoked it. Then she did the washing-up, and cut up some chips for tea. After that she lit another fag and stood smoking it beside the window.

Eventually curiosity overcame her reticence. She picked the notes up from the side and sat down at the kitchen table, counting them out.

25

I sat quietly and tried not to squirm. If I caught Nan's attention she might scream and break the spell. The cracker with the piece of cheese lay at my feet. I clenched my eyes tightly and screwed up my fists.

'Mouse,' I prayed hard. 'I want to be a mouse.'

I had been reading *The Tale of Two Bad Mice* that morning. It was an old, battered copy, Mum's book from when she was smaller than me. 'Katie Bainbridge, Age 6', it said on the flyleaf, in what must have been Nan's writing, or Grampy B's. The other pages were covered in faded pencil scrawls, circling lines produced by the tight grip of young, clammy hands.

'I want to be a mouse.'

I imagined, as hard as I could, that James and me were the two bad mice. James was back from his adventure. He was beside me, invisible with new magical powers and hidden from adult sight. We were playing the games that we always played.

'Mouse, mouse, mouse,' I heard him chant as I clenched my eyes tight.

Then it happened. It worked. A tingling sensation ripped through my whole body. My two front teeth pushed down, yellow fangs grazing the pink of my lower lips, my back arched up into the air, a tail thumped against the nape of my back, aching to get out, a fine white down covered my cheeks and my nose began to twitch uncontrollably.

Oblivious to my transformation, Nan continued to busy herself at the sink, submerging plates into the soapy water, wiping down sides and lugging the ironing board out from the cupboard and onto the kitchen floor. It was the wrong day, I wanted to tell her, ironing day was Monday, but then I remembered that I could only squeak, and focused instead on the cracker in front of me.

It was quiet in the house, after yesterday.

Quiet, like nothing had happened.

Or quiet, like everything had.

I crouched down on my paws and nibbled at the slices of cheese with my new long teeth. The skin around my newly sprouted whiskers felt sore, like spots. The cheese tasted slightly rubbery, and warm. The cracker splintered dusty fragments over the floor.

'Time for a cup of tea, I think,' Nan sighed. 'I suppose I should ask your father if he wants one.'

She wiped her hands with a tea towel and wandered into the living room, exchanging some words with Dick Roberts, but I was too preoccupied to listen. After a minute or so she re-entered the kitchen, glancing down at me as she passed through the door. Her eyes narrowed when she saw the mess on the floor.

'What are you playing at, you filthy bugger?' she snapped. 'Rolling around and making a mess like a five-year-old,' she said, grabbing my arm and pulling me up. 'It's a bloody disgrace. Get a cloth and wipe it up.'

She squeezed a dishcloth over the sink and handed it to me.

'I can't get my finger wet,' I squeaked, twitching my nose like a mouse should, holding up the bandage to remind her.

Nan sighed irritably and pushed me roughly out of the way, crouching to wipe the crumbs up herself. Her joints creaked.

'Your dad wants you in the living room anyway,' she grumbled.

The spell immediately burst, at that. The fur vanished from my face, my talons withered back into nails and the imaginary, makeshift James, for an instant so vivid, like a witch doused in water, shrivelled away from sight.

Nan looked up in time to catch the expression on my face. Her frown softened.

'It's all right, he won't bite,' she whispered in my ear, putting a hand on my shoulder to steady herself as she pulled herself from the carpet.

She gave me the ghost of a wink before she clipped me softly on the back of my head and pushed me towards the door.

'Go on, do as you're told.'

Dick Roberts was making one of his models. Mum bought him one every Christmas, a box full of matchstick pieces, a pallet of paints, a tube of glue and a set of directions on how to erect historical houses and monuments. He liked to fiddle with them in his spare time, when he wasn't down the Blackbird or watching the telly, and when I entered the living room, the half-started matchstick miniature of the Houses of

Parliament was set out on some old newspaper, on the floor in front of him. He'd been working on it for the past six months, ever since Boxing Day, Christmas last. He had sat on the floor then, with an orange Christmas cracker crown on his head, immersed in the instructions, the open box by his side, while we watched *Mary Poppins* on the telly. Occasionally his fingers would dip into the contents, rifling through the different bits and pieces.

He crouched beside it now, on all fours in his Saturday clothes, twisting his head around and surveying the work in progress from different angles. It didn't look much, at the moment, being only the foundations. Just neat little disappointing rows of glued matchsticks, no towers or turrets.

'Come on,' he said, patting the floor beside him when he saw me hesitating at the door. 'Come and help me out.'

'Here,' he continued, sliding the box towards me, 'the matchsticks are all mixed up; you sort them into sizes.'

The phone rang out in the hallway, and after two or three rings I heard Nan leave the kitchen and answer it.

'We'll have a go at Big Ben today, eh? You can paint some of the matchsticks if you like,' Dick Roberts said.

I nodded mutely.

He hardly looked at me. He was too busy examining the model. I sat quietly on the carpet, shuffling the matches into groups, while he mixed the glue together on a jam-jar lid, stirring the sticky substance with one of the tiny wooden sticks.

'Grab one of the cushions to sit on if you like,' he said, and I noticed as he cast a sly glance at the bandage on my finger.

He saw that I had seen him, and looked quickly away.

'That doesn't hurt too much now, does it?' he asked. I shook my head.

He smiled, placated, and went back to stirring the glue and scanning the instructions at his feet.

Nan came into the living room. She stopped at the sofa, resting her hands on it as she smiled at Dick, something that she never normally did. There was a look of profound relief on her face.

'That was the police,' she said. 'He's been found, round at the Pledges'.'

'What?' Dick Roberts said. His pale face blanched further white and he dropped the tube of glue to the floor, as his hands began to shake. 'The Pledges'? That's ... but that's only around the corner.'

'The mother found him. Up in the bedroom, with the youngest.'

'Just around the corner.'

'That's all they said.'

Nan stood there, taking a deep breath.

'All I know is that they're going to pick him up, and that he'll be home in half an hour,' she said. I could have sworn her eyes were a bit misty. 'That's good enough for me.'

26

When Mum had finished counting the money that Nan had given her, her brow wrinkled. She lit up a cigarette and smoked it, inhaling deeply, the movements furrowing the lines around her lips. After she'd finished she covered her eyes with her hands and leaned heavily on the table.

'Shit,' she whispered.

Then she counted the money out again, and then once more after that.

'How'd you know how much was missing?' she asked Nan the next day.

Nan's eyes flickered for a split second before she replied.

'You told me,' she said.

It must have been over a year later that the news of Grampy R's death came. Both women were in the same positions as they had been twelve months earlier sitting in the kitchen, taking a tea break, when the jangle of the telephone began to echo in from the hall.

'Must be Net phoning from the clinic,' Mum commented, hastily stubbing out the dog-end of her cigarette and hurrying to get it.

'You can tell her that I'm not going to go and see her,' Nan shouted after her. 'Tell her she's a bloody disgrace.'

But it wasn't Net. It was Uncle Rob. Nan R had wanted him to ring, he'd said, about Grampy R. Cancer, he said. They'd known for a while but hadn't wanted to worry anyone. A peaceful death, in his sleep.

The funeral was on Thursday.

'I had a funny feeling, you know,' Mum said, quietly, after she'd come back into the room and explained what had happened. 'I knew that something was wrong.'

Her eyes looked blank.

211

'I'll wait until Dick gets home to tell him,' she said. 'No point getting him out of work.'

She didn't sit down again, but walked over to the ironing she had been doing before. She reached blindly down into the basket with the rumpled clothes, pulling out socks and pants and shirts, pressing them down onto the board. It was a cheap board, and old. The pale flowers scattered over the protective cover were occasioned with deep brown blisters, and the frail criss-crossing legs rattled precariously whenever she pressed too hard.

They were rattling now.

Mum ironed and ironed. She didn't speak and she didn't look at Nan; she didn't even look up to thank her when Nan made her a cup of tea and placed it on a mat, on the sideboard.

The dishevelled red basket deflated and the pristine yellow basket, full of shirts, skirts, jumpers – all neatly folded and starched – on the other side of her legs, grew.

'Come on, I'll do some,' Nan offered after a while, getting up, but Mum ignored her. She picked up the water spray from the side and squirted at a stubborn crease.

'No,' she said, before stopping to wipe what might have been a tear from her eye.

'Oh, Katie,' Nan sighed, shaking her head as she sat back down. 'After all they've done to you?'

'Don't start.'

'Come on, love, sit down and have a cigarette with your old mum.'

Mum still didn't respond and Nan lit up by herself instead. She sat smoking, watching Mum and the hypnotic rhythm of her arm gliding left and right, up and down the board.

'Well, I hope you're not going to go, anyway.'

But Mum carried on ironing, methodically rolling the iron to and fro.

Only when the red clothes basket was empty did she turn and face Nan.

'You hope I'm not going to go where?'

'To the funeral.'

Mum looked hard at Nan, resting her arm on the ironing board for support. She licked her tongue over her front teeth and narrowed her tear-flushed eyes.

Then she spoke.

'I know what happened,' she said.

Nan's raised eyebrows slumped. Her contrary face paled for an instant before she pulled herself up sharply in her chair and struggled to regain her equilibrium.

'What do you mean?' she stuttered.

'Don't make me spell it out, Mum.'

She didn't. The two of them simultaneously reached for their cigarette packets.

Nan stared quietly out of the window.

'Will you look at that,' she murmured, after a while, adjusting her glasses and nodding at the crystal drops that had begun to splash against the pane. 'Bloody raining again, middle of summer as well.'

After a long pause Mum answered. She sighed, and stubbed out her cigarette.

'Sod's law,' she said, throwing Nan a short smile before she picked up the iron and unplugged it from the socket.

And that was that.

The money was never mentioned again, and neither were the Robertses.

It was almost as if they had never existed at all, that they had been figments of our imaginations, strange dreams that had only existed in the dark, and like other things that went bump in the night they had dissolved into the dawn.

Two

27

It was the second week back. Monday, half past three, five minutes after the final ring of the bell, with all the usual clamour that accompanied the end of the school day. I struggled with my cardigan, casting a glance at the sky as I picked my way through the blue throng, which clattered noisily out of the tall school gates. September: the cloud-thickening end of summer. Barney, the lollypop man, shouted with impatience as children raced across the road, ignoring him. A few horns beeped. I sidestepped a painting someone had dropped on the ground, a rough rendition of a house and a family and their cat, and waited for Barney before I crossed. A small boy from one of the lower years ran past me, hopping up onto the opposite pavement to grab the hand of his waiting mum, who stood talking to another woman.

Three girls from my new form slouched against a garden wall, their socks wrinkled around their ankles, their legs a blue-veined, skinny tangle of bruises and scabs. They eyed me lazily as I walked past. Sasha Brennan. Tanya and Tracey Best, the twins, who would have been indistinguishable if it weren't for the colours of their hair.

'Spamet,' Sasha, the biggest one, called after me, without much energy.

I didn't look round.

That's what they all called me. Spammy Janny. Spamet. Put-a-can-in-it, Janet.

I carried on walking instead, up Cumberland Road, not in the direction of home but the other way, past the dirty white council flats, past the bus terminus, where a middle-aged man sat alone, looking sad and drinking something from a brown paper bag, up to the junction and left onto Cuddeston Way, passing groups of older children dressed in different uniforms, towards Wesley Green, James's new – grown-up – middle school.

James was there, in the playground, luckily enough.

I heard his shout before I saw him. He let out a jubilant whoop, and I turned in time to see him dodge Pledgie's lethargic keeping and score a goal. The football shot past Pledgie's legs. It crashed into the fence behind him, before springing off it and tumbling down the path towards me.

'There's only one Kevin Keegan,' James yelled, punching his fists in the air before taking a deep bow.

They were on the small playing field, the four of them, having a bit of a kick-around before the teachers on after-school play-ground duty turfed them out. It wasn't a real football pitch, just a dirty square of grass. They had used their bags to set out the goalposts.

A couple of girls I didn't recognize stood to one side, watching the boys through veiled eyes and chattering softly to one another. One of them, the one with a high brown ponytail and a smear of deep lipstick and a gold chain around her neck – which arched gracefully from the daringly open buttons of her white school shirt – lifted one foot up and scratched a calf, idly, as she talked. 'Yeah,' she said, through chewing gum rotations. 'I know what you mean. Definitely.' The other girl whispered something else and she nodded again and said, 'Better get a move on, I s'pose.' And she gave the boys one final stare before slinging her bag over her shoulder and moving off, with her dumpier, altogether spottier friend, past me and through the Cuddeston Way gates.

I sidled over and hovered near one of the goalposts.

They carried on playing. James mainly kept the ball to himself. Neil and Danny occasionally jumped in with half-hearted tackles, but James was quick to get the ball back, either legitimately or by tripping them up. When he did that they picked themselves off the ground, wiping the mud off their grey trousers and shouting, though limply, it seemed, without much hope of being heard, 'Foul!'

Danny Jones.

Neil Bushnell.

Richard Pledge.

I knew all of them. They lived close together, in the streets to the back of our house. Danny and Neil lived in Bullrush Place, which was behind Hazelnut Path, off Field Avenue. Field Avenue was where Pledgie lived. They sometimes played rounders and cricket in the sports field. Neil was small and lean with mousy hair and castoff clothes and a nose too big for his face. Danny was half Jamaican, small again, cleaner and neater and quieter than either Neil or Richard Pledge. He said things like please and thank you and seemed to think before he spoke. He was Colin's son. Colin worked up The Works with Dick Roberts, on the same line, and everyone –well, Nan and Mum – conceded that, though they weren't as a rule so keen on coloured people, Colin was all right.

'He's been here so long,' Nan said. 'He'd be the first to admit that he's practically white.'

The football shot past me, narrowly missing my legs, as James misfired a goal.

He cast a glance my way as he ran to retrieve the ball, but didn't say anything.

'Goal kick,' he shouted to the others and, rolling the ball to Pledgie, jogged back over the grass.

A few other boys came over to join them and they played on, shouting and jostling each other. I felt a sudden chill as the sun moved behind a cloud. The game grew more boisterous and I edged away from the goalpost, turning to take a look around me. Wesley Green Middle School. It was a shabby collage of red brick. Ugly square buildings, with dark, vast windows and peeling window sills. There was a scattering of Portakabins too. Their panels were daubed with graffiti and their temporary existence was accentuated by the dirty brick-stilts they balanced on, though in the main –

or so the local adults said – those Porta-kabins had lasted longer than the teachers ever had.

'Two nil!' someone shouted.

There was a brief cheer before another boy shouted, 'Offside!'

I watched as they stopped playing, crowding round to argue, Pledgie ambling across from the goal, oblivious to the teacher who had appeared at the far edge of the grass until he blew loudly on a whistle.

They looked round.

'Come on,' the teacher shouted. There was a no-nonsense quality to his tone. 'Get a move on, you lot. This isn't a social club.'

The boys groaned, but did what they were told.

James walked over and bent to pick up his crumpled school jacket, using one of the sleeves to wipe his forehead. His face was hot with sweat, his armpits were dark with moisture and his hair was sticking to his skin.

'What you doing here, Flid?' he asked, at last looking up at me.

'Nan says you're supposed to come and get me after school,' I mumbled, focusing on my shoes, avoiding his gaze and the looks of his three new friends as they began to gather around, packing up and putting on their coats.

'So? She's not my mum. Who's she to tell me what to do?'

'You've got to do what she says, while Mum's away.'

'What you going to do, make me?'

'You coming, James?'

It was Richard Pledge. He stood with the others, ready to leave, looking as large as ever with his towering gait and his oversized head. 'Frankenstein,' older boys called him, on account of his forehead, which was enormous. Everything about him, in fact, was big. Big freckles splayed across his big cheeks, his thick mouth frequently widened into a gaping grin. With his height and bulky body, he must have been the largest of the new first years. They all called him Hulk, after the Incredible Hulk.

I knew what 'coming?' referred to. They'd been going there every day after school for the past week – up to the shops by the bridge, at the edge of the estate, to play pre-rush hour Chicken Across The Road. Different groups of them hung round outside the chippy, from after school until late at night, for as long as they were allowed. The younger ones mainly just played around outside but the older ones, those who did paper rounds and had money to spare, bought large, greasy bags of chips and cans of Coke, and played on the fruit machine and pinball game.

James shrugged. He swung his carrier bag over his shoulder with the same studied insouciance of the girl, earlier.

'Nah,' he said.

'Come on, just for ten minutes.'

'I got to go and see my mum.'

'Can't you see her tomorrow?'

They started to move, pausing again just outside the gates. Pledgie knotted his school tie around his brow, like a sports sweatband, then took it off again and stuffed it in his pocket. He started to bounce his football on the pavement, up, down, up, down.

'Come on. We're going over to Danny's later.'

'Yeah. He got a new game from the market yesterday. Jet Set Willy. Didn't you, Dan?'

But James just shook his head, saying I can't, can I?

He ignored Pledgie's further come ons, and gave them their special, secret gang salute.

'Until tomorrow,' he said.

'Until tomorrow.'

'Until tomorrow.'
'Until tomorrow.'
We watched as the three of them dawdled down the road, away from us, past the scout hut and the ugly Holy Family church. They turned, giving a final wave, before rounding the corner and disappearing from sight. James dropped his hand and turned to me.

'What you looking at?' he said.

I shrugged.

'Come on, let's go.'

And so we walked home – James ten paces ahead – taking a short cut over the sports field. A few drops of rain splattered against my face and legs. Our house, at first just a matchstick-box in the distance, grew bigger and bigger with each step, until soon it was there, right in front of us. We climbed through the gap in the railings, crossed the road and swung through the creaking gate, up to the door.

'Hold on,' Nan called from the kitchen.

We stood, waiting for her to let us in.

28

Aunty Net rapped on the window as I passed hers the following day. She must have been waiting, specially. I looked around and saw the side of the curtains flitter. Her pale face appeared at the smudged window pane, and then the nets dropped into place.

'I've got to get home,' I called, but she didn't seem to have heard me when she finally emerged.

'Hello, darling,' she breathed, limping up the garden path.

She looked pale and tired, although she was smiling. Her arms were folded tightly over a bottle, but it was only lemon barley water.

'Give this to your mum, will you?' she asked, handing it to me. 'You are going up, later?'

'In a bit.'

'Well, give her that and send her my love.'

I nodded, muttering something about needing to get home for tea, but again she didn't seem to hear me.

'How was she, yesterday?'

'I dunno.'

'What do you mean, you don't know?'

'Only Nan and Dad went. We didn't go.'

'What did you do?'

'We stayed at home.'

'Oh ... I thought you'd gone up with them.'

She sat down on the wall – on the small section that was still in place – and cast her fingers over her face. I sat down beside her. She didn't look very well. You never could quite tell with Aunty Net, but it looked as though she might have been crying. The patterned skirt she was wearing was coming apart at the seams, and nasty pink and white blotches of psoriasis crawled up her legs. There was a hole in the toe of her slipper and I could see her calloused, dirty toenail jutting out of it.

'I don't suppose you've got five minutes, to keep your old aunty company?'

'Not really.'

'Only I got some bad news yesterday. I don't feel like sitting inside all by myself.'

'Nan's waiting for me.'

She nodded at that, and didn't say any more. We sat, watching the road. A number 52 drove past – its destination the train station, right up in town. I'd only been there once, that time we had gone to see Nan and Grampy R in Leigh-on-Sea. The bus went right through the centre of Oxford to get there, past the vast colleges with their gold-handed clocks and leering gargoyles.

'I don't know if I can take much more of it,' Aunty Net murmured.

She took her fingers from her cheeks and gazed over at the last, scattered groups of schoolchildren walking by. I wriggled uncomfortably, saying nothing. The bricks were hard against the back of my legs. Manilow strolled, leopard-like, along the path, and curled himself around my ankles. I leaned down to stroke him and he purred, rubbing his chin against my hand. A brown bird flew from a rooftop and into the Hornet Swatting Tree.

'I better get going, Aunty Net.'

'What?'

'I better get going.'

Aunty Net blinked once, twice. She patted me on the head before standing up.

'Never mind. Having a bad day, that's all,' she said, clenching her arms back around her tiny middle. 'Go on then, you had better get on home before that old bitch starts having a go.'

I nodded, and she smiled weakly. She threw me a little wave and turned on her heel, ducking her chin as she hobbled up the pot-holed pathway and disappeared back through her front door, pulling it shut.

'Where's that brother of yours?' Nan said as soon as she opened our door.

'I don't know.'

She was looking at me like it was my fault.

'What do you mean you don't know? Didn't you wait for him, like I told you to?'

'He wasn't there.'

'I'll be having words with that little scallywag when he gets back. He's getting too big for his boots,' she grumbled. Her eyes fell on the bottle I was holding. 'What's that?'

Dick Roberts was wearing his suit. It was his new one, a flimsy grey affair Mum had ordered from Freeman's. In the catalogue the man that wore it looked like a tanned, muscular colleague of James Bond. She must have felt a momentary flash of disappointment when she saw Dick Roberts in it for the first time, modelling his new acquisition in the kitchen – not bronzed, not rippling, no toothpaste advert, easy smiles, but standing thin and pale – struggling clumsily with his sterling silver cufflinks, frowning.

He clacked down the corridor in front of us. His black polished shoes tapped against the shiny white tiles and the sound rebounded, tinny, off the walls. Nan walked beside him, her beige leather handbag clutched purposefully in one hand and a carrier bag of magazines, green grapes and barley water in the other. Her new blue chiffon scarf was wrenched firmly around her head. It accentuated her nose, which protruded, grandly, from the frame of it.

Mum had come into hospital for some tests. She told us that she'd be gone the whole week, right up until Friday, and that Nan was going to look after us and we had to behave ourselves. She said the doctors had to do a biopsy and figure out just how far 'it' had spread. She didn't say what 'it' was, and we knew better than to ask.

Occasionally Dick Roberts's hand flew up to scratch his hair, or tug at his collar and tie.

Every now and again Nan looked around at us. She had that warning look on her face: the one that said there'd be hell to pay if we stepped out of line. She'd told us to stay together and hold hands. James did what he was told, probably because of the ear bending she'd given him when he'd eventually trailed in from school. He was trying his hardest to dig his nails into my skin.

I didn't like the hospital. Everything was clean and yet at the same time in a state of decline. The shiny floor tiles were grooved with the erosion of trolleys and feet. White paint peeled off the wall plaster like old scabs from skin. And it smelled – already dead. It was a strange combination of things, a dissipating cocktail made up on the one hand from the scents of illness: faeces, sweat and iron, stale dribble. That was the foundation. The second layer was artificial, non-human: disinfectants and medications, substances used to kill one thing in the hope of waking another.

I didn't like it. It made me feel a bit sick.

'It's like a bloody maze in here,' Nan said, to no one in particular.

James dug his nails further into my palm. I flinched, and tried to pull my hand away.

'Stop it,' I whispered.

White uniformed nurses moved noise-lessly up and down the corridors, pausing to talk to each other or murmur purposefully to white-coated doctors with long, tired faces. Sometimes the corridors opened out into wards full of patients. Some lay in bed, passively attached to large machines that ticked and whirred menacingly. A couple of times their eyes caught mine as I passed. I felt shivers of fright then, and looked away. Other patients had visitors, who, for the most part, sat beside the beds looking bored, melancholy and dazed. Some read the magazines they had originally brought as presents, most hadn't removed their coats. Few spoke.

James dug his nails a third time. I twisted my hand free and pinched his wrist.

'I'll tell Nan you've been smoking,' I whispered, bringing my free fingers up to my lips to imitate a smoking motion, as we rounded another corner.

'Albion ward.' Nan stopped, squinting up at the sign above her head. 'Here we go.'

She turned round to us and stooped, licking her finger and cleaning some grime off James's cheek. He pouted but she didn't stop.

'I don't want to hear a peep out of you two,' Dick Roberts said. His face had assumed the odd quality of looking both paler and darker at the same time. He tugged his tie and glared at the limp bodies around him, the prone people and the nametags. I saw his Adam's apple bobbing up and down.

Nan struggled to straighten up. She had

stooped further than she needed to, perhaps from some subconscious element of pride – because she didn't want to admit that James had suddenly started to grow again, and would soon be nearing her height. After she'd caught her breath, she walked over to the counter where some nurses were sitting.

'We're here to see Katherine Bainbridge,' she said, putting on her best voice.

'Roberts – Katherine Roberts,' Dick Roberts interjected.

He shuffled uncomfortably, and went back to fiddling with his tie. I followed his gaze, over to the quadrant of beds' opposite the desk. Two of the beds were cordoned with green, flower-patterned curtains, but in the ones closest to us, two old women lay, with greasy salt and pepper hair, and creased skin and dark eyes that grazed the ceiling. Coloured tubes zoomed in and out of them.

One of the nurses walked us over to one of the cordoned beds, saying that Mum had been moved, earlier, because it turned out that two of the other ladies were actually neighbours and wanted beds next to each other.

She popped her head into the curtain, saying, 'Hello, Mrs Roberts, I've got some visitors here for you. Isn't that nice?'

Then she drew the drapes back, and there was Mum.

She half sat, half lay in bed, with her black hair extra black against the pillow white.

'All right, then?' she managed, before giving way to a gentle little cough.

'All right, luvvie?' Nan said, sitting in the one visitors' chair and pulling out the various items from the carrier bag.

Dick Roberts busied himself, scraping another chair across the ward floor.

Mum glanced over to where we stood.

'What's the matter with you two, cat got your tongues?'

'I've got you your *Woman's Weekly*,' Nan was saying, 'and a couple of those word search books you like. Annette sent you up some barley water.'

She put the bottle and the grapes on the side cabinet, and the magazine and books on Mum's bed, and started to undo her scarf.

'I'd go careful though. I wouldn't put it past her to spike it with a bit of vodka.'

'Don't start, Mum. You haven't been here two minutes.'

'Well. You never can tell with that silly cow. Doo-bloody-lally.'

'What's the news on Stan's car? Found who took it, yet?'

'Don't think so. I haven't heard anything.'

They slipped into banter, while Dick Roberts flicked through the *Sun*. We sat on the cold tiled floor, me with an Enid Blyton and James with a comic book. I looked up at Mum every now and then. She didn't look any different: she was wearing her own nightie and chattering away to Nan, not minding us, just like she did at home. It seemed normal, almost; I wouldn't say it felt like home, but it was near enough.

A clock hung over the nurses' desk. The black plastic minute hand slowly edged its way around. People – staff, visitors – came and went, cluttering up the wards and the air with their tick-tacking shoes and their talk, and our visit clicked on.

29

'What do you think he's playing at?' James said, later that night, using one of Nan's favourite phrases.

'What do you mean?'

He was wearing his Spiderman pyjamas. He'd got them at Christmas, but by now the trousers were too short and ended above his ankles. His right index finger was stuffed up his right nostril. He was sitting on my bunk. Well, my old bunk. Mum had been so pleased when he'd returned home safe and sound that she had said he could swap with me and have the top bunk almost before he'd finished asking her. She told me not to be so selfish when I complained, and asked – disapprovingly – whether I wasn't pleased to have my big brother home again.

'Yes,' I'd said.

'Well,' she'd replied. 'Take that look off your face and start acting like it.'

'I mean,' James said, wiping his finger on the quilt cover, 'letting us sit in the living room, and all that.'

What he said was true. We were being allowed in the living room, suddenly. We were allowed to take in our colouring pencils and books, and everything. It was all back to front somehow: Nan was playing Mum and James was being horrible and Dick Roberts was being – almost – OK. Almost. Not a Nan or Mum OK, admittedly, but a peculiar type of Dick Roberts OK. A come and sit in the living room – in silence – kind of OK; a watch these television programmes with me but don't make any noise and don't ask any questions.

'He's hardly hit us for weeks now.'

'That's because he's scared of Mum.'

'Hardly.'

'Mum had a go at him when you ran away.'

I'd told him before, but he wouldn't believe me.

'I swear. She smashed a bottle and shook it in his face.'

'You're making it up.'

'Ask Nan. She'll tell you.'

James was silent. He carried on picking his nose, and I looked over to the window. There was a gap in the curtains, and dust played in a shard of dimming silver light.

'He wouldn't touch me now,' James said.

'Why not?'

'He's scared of me.' I snorted.

'Well, he hasn't hit me, has he? Not since I got back.'

'It's only because the police came round.'

'He's scared of me.'

'He's not, he's scared of Nan.'

'You just said it was Mum he was scared of. Make your mind up.'

I reached over and jabbed him, but he only

237

moved further across the bed, telling me not to touch what I couldn't afford. That was another one of his and Pledgie's little sayings. I could picture them, snickering together, like they did every time they tried out a new one. They made up nicknames for everyone, too. Neil's was 'Neil Neil Orange Peel' – or 'Gyppo' because he couldn't afford new clothes and always had to wear his elder brothers' outgrown stuff. Danny's was 'Fanny' and 'Pussy Gaylord', because he was such a poof, and mine was just 'Flid'. They hadn't got around to Mum or Nan, but they called Dick Roberts 'Dickhead', 'Dick by name, Dick by nature' and 'Dick the Prick'. These were good nicknames for him, I had to admit, but I couldn't help noticing how tired Dick Roberts looked lately – caved-in, like a wind-punched sail.

'Get off my bed, anyway.'

'It's my bed really.'

'No, it's not. It's mine now. Get off. I don't want your lurgy hands all over my stuff. I might catch something.'

He started pushing me. He had that new, sour look on his face, the one he'd developed since he'd been back home and started hanging round Richard Pledge. The expression he used when he remembered that, actually, I was just a girl and a younger one at that, and he wasn't supposed to enjoy talking to me.

'Get off, dog breath.'

I slapped his hands away, and slithered off the side, feeling with my toes for my mattress.

'All right, I'm going. Keep your hair on.'

'Good. And don't come back.'

I won't, I thought. I pulled back the covers to my bed and slipped beneath the warm flannel sheet. The mattress springs creaked above me as he did the same. I could hear him, imitating me: keep your hair on, keep your hair on. I don't care, I thought to myself. I watched as the light behind the curtains dimmed to its final grey, and night set in.

'Night,' I said, but he didn't answer me.

30

'Here.' Pledgie plucked his hand from his trouser pocket and threw three bent, slightly grubby cigarettes down onto the damp floor.

'Spastic,' James snapped, hurriedly retrieving them. 'It's wet. You'll ruin them.'

He squinted challengingly at Pledgie and Danny and Neil before dropping the fags into his pocket.

'Besides, we're not allowed to smoke them until we've sorted this place out for winter.'

We were standing in the dried-out ditch behind Bullrush Place, at the very edge of our part of the estate. There was only farmland beyond, sprawling fields of stubble where there had, so Pledgie said, a few weeks before, been wheat. I'd never seen the farmer – in fact, I'd never been into the ditch before this, and didn't even often remember that these fields were nearby – but Pledgie said he had, and that he was fat and ugly and had chased him once with a gun and his dog, which had rabies and drooled white spit. I wondered what he thought of us. It can't have been nice, having to stand and watch as our concrete ghetto threatened to sweep into his golden grasses, like a poisonous, urban lava. Perhaps that was the function of the ditch: it acted as a kind of thin buffer zone, a trench dividing our concrete world from the farmer's rural one.

You got to the ditch by lowering yourself through a spiky tangle of hedge, which cut across the end of Bullrush Place, curtailing the onset of houses. Mostly people seemed to use it as a dump. There was lots of rubbish; among other things I could see a rusting trolley and a mangy blue mattress with its springs sticking out, leaking brown rust. It smelled nasty, musty, a bit like old man's pee. It might have been all right in the summer, but now it was getting too damp. Ivy curled up the arthritic, stunted tree limbs, marred with blackening spots; the ground was muddy from the rain. There were logs but they were sodden, and left a curdled green smudge on my skirt when I tried to sit down.

The boys seemed to like it, though. They had brought James to see it (and by proxy me, because Nan had put her foot down yesterday and said he could only go out and play if he took me with him), forsaking the usual trip up to the chippy. They showed it to him proudly, and told him how they had messed around a bit in it over the summer, how it was well hidden, how it might make a good camp.

'Come on, what are you waiting for? We need to tidy it all up,' James said. He started to wrench up the mattress but dropped it quickly, saying, 'Ugh!' and wiping his hand down his trousers.

'What if we don't want to sort it out?' Neil Bushnell grumbled.

Pledgie gave him a small push and said, 'Shut your face, Gyppo.'

I didn't know the Bushnell family all that well, though Nan was on speaking terms with them. They were poor, poorer than the rest of us even. We all lived in the same style of house but there were eight of them, and only three bedrooms. There was the mum and the dad and six sons. Their dad had worked with our dad, up at The Works, but then he'd had an accident with some machinery and got laid off. Dick Roberts came home and told us about it, the day it happened. He said that Frank Bushnell's arm had been caught and crushed. He had seen it all, had heard the sound of Frank's bones crunching. He said that Frank had turned white and passed out cold from the shock of it, and that when he came to he couldn't say a thing. Their mum didn't work either. I'd hardly ever seen her. The times I had, she was being pushed up to the doctor's surgery by one of her sons, or going to church. Not the Holy Family Church – the Sacred Heart Church, which was up past Cuddeston Way, behind James's school and near the dog track. You would see the lot of them then, boys and men of varying ages, processing up the road in their Sunday clothes with their mum at the helm, a funny sort of wheelchaired figurehead, and their one-armed, whisky-cheeked dad limping along beside her. Nan would wave if she was out and they walked past, but in private she would say that she didn't trust Catholics, not as far as she could throw them. It reeked of black magic to her, all that incense and Holy Mary stuff. And she told Mum that the Irish patron saint was the patron saint of thieves. But they didn't look like thieves to me. They never had new clothes for a start. I glanced over at Neil. The jumper he was wearing was too big for him, old and frayed: not stolen goods but a stripy cast-off, as usual, from one of his brothers – who had probably got it from a charity shop in the first place.

'Don't call me a gyppo,' he was saying.

'What you going to do, stop me?'

'Yeah. G-I-P-O.'

I crouched, off to one side, using a twig to scribble words in the ground.

Janet Annette Bainbridge. Aged 8¾. Cumberland First School.

The mud glinted with different colours of

broken glass. Occasionally my twig caught on the hard edge of one of the fragments.

'You going to stop us?'

'Might do, Frankenstein.'

'What?'

'*Frankenstein.* That's your name, isn't it, Franky?'

I couldn't help but admire him. He just sat on, defiantly picking at tiny tufts of mud on his trousers, studiously nonchalant, ignoring the look on Pledgie's face. I knew the silence meant bad news, and so did he, but he didn't budge.

James and Pledgie grouped together, sliding over the ground towards one another, like a pair of sly hyenas.

The chant rose like a low hiss.

James started it.

'At least my mum's not in a wheelchair.'

'At least my mum's not in a wheelchair, at least my mum's not in a wheelchair, at least–'

It worked. Neil remained sitting, but it didn't take long before his dirty face scrunched into a ball of pain. He succumbed, jumped up and lurched towards James. But James was too quick: he grabbed Neil by his hair before he could do anything, and yanked him backwards. Neil fell sharply to the ground.

'We've got our own clothes! We don't get leftovers in our packed lunch!'

They rolled around. Dropping his bag, Pledgie sprang forward and leaped onto the writhing bundle.

'Get off me, you fat fuck!'

'Fishfinger sandwiches!'

Danny hadn't joined in. He stood to one side, uneasily scuffing his heels in the mud, trying not to watch and looking up instead, through the gaggle of diseased branches, at the approaching storm. I glanced up with him. The weather hadn't cleared since yesterday. Black clouds were re-gathering. The motley greys clashed against the dark greens and ambers of the leaves. The blank air began to fill with cold.

I shivered, pulling my school cardigan tightly around my chest.

'My mum'll kill me.' Neil, defeated, disentangled himself from the thrashing mass.

'How can she kill you when she can't even stand up to catch you?'

Neil froze, but then shrugged resignedly and clambered up from the ground, brushing himself down. The three of them looked at their clothes. James sat down on one of the logs. He held out his hand just as the first, tear-shaped raindrops began to fall.

'We could've had a fag, but it's too wet now,' he said.

'No, it's all right – it's only spitting. We'll just hold our hands over them, like this.' Pledgie cupped his hands together, over his mouth.

'All right, then.'

The three boys hunched together and struggled with some matches. Eventually they managed to light one, and sat, coughing and spluttering, as they passed the cigarette from hand to hand.

'Ugh, it's horrible.'

'No, not like that. You've got to breathe in, haven't you?'

'Where did you get them from, anyway?' James asked Pledgie. His face had assumed a funny shape as he struggled not to cough, and keep his cool.

'From my mum's handbag.'

'Didn't she catch you?'

'Nah. She don't count them.'

'But what if she does?'

'She'll just think that it's Mark nicking them,' Pledgie reasoned. He swivelled his head, looking round to where Danny stood.

'You've got to have a drag as well,' he said.

Danny shook his head.

'You've got to.'

'I don't fancy it. Thanks, though.'

'Come on, Pussy. You've got to, if you want to stay in our gang.'

'Leave him alone. It's more for us, anyway.'

They didn't bother asking me.

'Let's save the other ones for Saturday, so we know we'll have some.'

'All right.'

The first cigarette finished, the boys sat together, looking sullen as more drops of rain splashed down.

'What shall we do?'

'It's raining. I might go home.'

'Let's play Murder Amber Jenkins,' Pledgie suggested.

For the first time, they squinted in my direction. My twig froze on 'Jan–', but then Neil saved me.

'Why is it always you two who get to tell us what to do?' he glowered.

He flicked out his foot, using the opportunity to kick James in the ankle. Pledgie reached out and slapped him. Neil scowled but didn't hit back, and they fell silent again. The raindrops began to scatter more fiercely, but luckily the trees sheltered us, and we didn't bother to move.

'Won't she be rotting by now?'

'Who?'

'Amber.'

'My dad said that they had to do an autopsy on her,' Danny joined in.

He sat down on the log with the others. Pledgie shrugged. I could tell he didn't know what autopsy meant.

'That's when they cut you up, isn't it?' I offered. 'Shut your face, Flid-mo. Who said you could talk?'

'She's right,' Danny said. He reached up and shook a branch, experimentally. A small cascade of water fell down. 'They cut you open to get clues. And they keep you in a freezer until they're finished.'

'What about the other girl that got murdered?' Neil asked.

'They don't even know her name, do they?'

'How can you bury someone if you don't know their name?'

'Who cares?'

'My mum said she was a prostitute,' Neil said. 'She said that Amber Jenkins was a prossie too. She said it was a punishment from God.'

They paused, reflecting on this new

information and the addition of a deity into the equation. I got up and picked up my bag. The rain and all the talk about Amber Jenkins and the Killer was making me shiver.

'You shouldn't say things like that; she might come back and haunt you.'

Pledgie turned to James.

'Why's your sister talking? She's only allowed to come if she keeps quiet.'

'Yeah. I thought we said no girls, anyway?'

'Nan'll be back by now,' I mumbled, looking over at James. 'She'll kill us if we come home soaked.'

Nan had gone up to the hospital earlier that afternoon on her own – she said that hospitals weren't places for kids and anyway, the bus fare was too expensive for us to go with her every single day. She had decided we could stay out and play until she got back though, and in that way she was much more lenient than Mum ever was.

'Why do you have to do what your nan says all the time?'

I stood awkwardly, ignoring him, waiting for James to reply. James scowled and wrinkled his nose at Pledgie, but was saved from an answer by a sudden downpour. The boys jumped up from the log, and we clambered hurriedly through the hole in the hedge: James first, Pledgie second, then Neil, then Danny, then me.

There was a gust of hailstones and a large crack of thunder. I skidded on a puddle and blinked rapidly, trying to see where I was going. The ice stung. A little trickle of blood, probably a scratch from a thorn in the hedge, dissolved into pink on my calf and ran down into my sock. Neil, in front, splashed through a puddle and sent a fresh shower of dirty water over my skirt and legs.

'Watch it!' I shouted, but nobody heard.

The boys shot through gateposts, one by one, into their various homes, until it was just James and I running, over the grass of Hazelnut Path, past Grampy R's blossom tree, past Nan's flats and the garages, round the corner to Cumberland Road.

31

Dinner was hot chips, a rasher of bacon and a fried egg. Nan had looked slightly abashed at the offering. She started to mutter something apologetic about not having had time to knock up anything better. Then she remembered herself and, giving us a look like we'd been the ones complaining, grumbled that she only had one pair of hands, after all.

'I'm not the Bionic Woman, you know.'

I didn't mind. I liked it. I smothered my chips in salt and malt vinegar and dabbed a blob of ketchup in between the rasher and the egg, nice and neatly, so it wasn't touching either.

The rain had cleared up and a rainbow was visible from the kitchen window, bright against the cracked grey of the clouds.

I speared one of the chips with my fork and plunged it into the egg, cutting through the thin skin and releasing the runny, sunny yolk.

James sat on the other side of the table, pouting his way through his food. I went to prod him with my foot but then thought better of it, remembering what he'd been like recently.

Dick Roberts was next to me. He'd got half a tin of beans with his dinner, too. He'd changed out of his wet overalls when he got home from work, and they had joined our sodden uniforms in the washing machine, which was from the catalogue, like most other things, and was paid for in instalments, little by little, week by week. It sloshed and whirred now, busy in the corner, as we continued to eat.

'Not long now,' Dick Roberts said, in between a mouthful of bacon and a forkful of beans. 'She'll be back on Friday.'

I glanced up, checking Nan's reaction. She carried on eating.

The washing machine started to rattle as it switched into spin, juddering so that James's school bag, which had been slung on top, hopped over the surface and fell to the carpet.

James pulled back his chair to go and pick it up, but Nan told him to leave it.

Dick Roberts cleared his throat.

'That will be good, won't it?' he asked.

It started out as a general question, I think, but he caught my eye as he said it. I stopped chewing, and nodded, holding my cutlery uncertainly over my plate. He noticed.

'It's all right,' he said. 'Go on, get it down you.'

It was just that we weren't normally allowed to talk at the kitchen table.

And it was Wednesday.

'What about you?' he asked James. 'What did you get up to at school?'

James shrugged. Dick Roberts waited. Nan finished eating and got up, carrying her plate over to the sink. She turned on the hot water and squirted a bit of Fairy into the washing-up bowl. Still, James didn't say anything.

'Come on,' Dick Roberts said, his voice betraying some of its usual impatience. 'Answer the question. Where are your manners?'

'Nothing much.'

'That's better.'

He looked down, busied himself slicing another piece of bacon. For a second it looked as though that was it, but then he started up again, speaking with his mouth full so that a small piece of potato popped out and stuck to his bottom lip.

'And you?'

I looked at him, sideways.

'Nothing much either, Janet?'

I nodded. That was right. Nothing much either. An image of my classroom flashed across my mind – the rows of tables, flimsy and chipped, what was left of their veneered surfaces messy with blue biroed scrawl; the beige walls, blotchy with fingerprints and greasy Blu-Tack stains, pocked with draw-ing-pin pores. Mrs Foster, this afternoon, reading slowly from *Charlotte's Web*, trying her best to bring the characters to life with different voices; having to break off with increasing frequency, to check all the giggles and whispers. Mrs Foster had short grey curly hair and a dainty cascade of double chins. She wrote with a silver fountain pen, and had to put up with what Nan would call a fair bit of lip.

'What did you have for lunch, then?'

'Ham sandwiches.'

'That all?'

'And a Penguin.'

'That's all right, then.'

I nodded.

'Nice to have a Penguin. Something sweet.'

Across the room, Nan switched the radio on. It was 'Every Breath You Take'. She turned it off, and plucked a tea towel for the drying up. Dick Roberts carried on eating his dinner without saying anything more. He left the room as soon as he'd finished, kicking back his chair and leaving the plate for Nan or us to clear away.

Nan watched him go.

She caught my eye as she came over to pick up the plate from the table, and raised her eyebrows.

'Egg and chips not good enough for some people?'

'Yes,' I muttered, hastily spearing another chip.

It was cold. I chewed on it slowly, eyeing the remaining food. The egg yolk was congealed, by now. It had developed a greasy, shiny film, and the bacon looked all damp and shrivelled. I stabbed my fork into the egg, tentatively. The prongs left a yellow-clawed swipe.

'You'll have to eat it. It's probably full of germs by now,' James whispered spitefully, then he broke off to look round as the front gate suddenly whined, swinging open and shut.

It was Neil Bushnell. Nan watched him from the window.

'What does he want?' she asked, as the doorbell went.

'He said he might come round after tea,' James said, shovelling in his last couple of chips, 'to see if I could go out.'

'Don't speak with your mouth full.'

'Sorry.'

Nan picked up a plate.

She stood, carefully wiping it before placing it on top of the stack of others, on the side.

'I don't want that Pledge boy here. He's not coming round and upsetting your mother, you hear? That boy's caused enough trouble as it is.'

James stuck his lip out, but gave a quick nod.

'I know all about that family,' Nan said. She picked up a saucepan.

James got up and took his things over to the sink. 'Can I go out? Just for a bit?'

'Go on then – but only out the front, where I can see you. And you can take your sister with you.'

'*But*–'

'But what?'

'Do I have to?'

'Do you want to go out, or not?'

32

'What's her name?'

'Beryl.'

We were outside our house, counting cars. Pledgie was blue, Neil grey, Danny white and James red. Pledgie was sitting on the ground against the garage wall (to the right of our house), so that Nan couldn't see him. James had picked the colours – deliberately, I thought, because there were plenty of red cars going by. I'd had to ask for a colour, they wouldn't give me one at first. Eventually they'd said I could have yellow. Everybody knew there weren't any yellow cars. They probably didn't even make them.

'She's old,' Neil said.

Pledgie shrugged.

'Yeah, but she's all right, though.'

It was still and peaceful. Nobody walked by. There was a mild, smoky, autumn-and-petrol scent in the early evening air. The rainbow had disappeared, but bright stripes of sunlight cut through the clouds. Down the road, the leaves of the Hornet Swatting Tree were starting to turn. It occurred to me that we hadn't bothered to swat any insects this year.

James, Neil and Danny sat on the wall. I balanced on the gate but didn't swing on it, in case it annoyed Nan and she called me in. Pledgie sat on the damp concrete, torment-ing a worm with a twig he'd picked up. I watched as it wriggled helplessly on the ground. It was long and brown, pleated with tiny rings that looked like fingerprints. Fragile. Pledgie's arm hovered for a moment and then slashed through the air, chopping the worm roughly in two. It kept on moving, the two halves flipping tortuously.

'Stop it!'

'What you going to do about it, Flid?' Pledgie glowered up at me. When I didn't answer, he turned his attention to James, switching the subject back to social workers. He liked talking about them. He thought he knew all about them. 'They've probably got you on their danger list. A register, it's called. Because of your dad and yon running away and everything.'

'*Shh!* You've got to whisper. He might hear you and then I'll be in for it.'

Pledgie and Neil's social worker was called Beryl Evans. According to them, she did most of the kids on Blackbird Leys. She had a car of her own and would sometimes take Pledgie and Neil out for drives in it.

'How come you need a social worker?' James asked Neil. 'Your dad's all right.'

'Yeah, but my mum's got MS.'

'S'pose.'

Neil picked up a piece of gravel and threw it up in the air, above his head. He didn't manage to catch it and didn't bother to pick it up again when it fell past his hand, back to the ground. I watched him, wondering what MS was.

'What about you?' he asked James.

'What?'

'What about your mum?'

He took care not to look at him as he said it.

James scowled. 'What about her?'

'Well, she's in hospital, isn't she? So she can't be very well, either.'

'So?'

'What's the matter with her? Is she dying?'

'Shut up.'

'Yeah, but–'

'Shut up!'

James punched Neil hard, on the thigh. Neil leaped up, clutching his leg, shouting, 'Get lost!'

James shrugged. 'Serves you right,' he said.

The others didn't say anything, and after a final hop Neil sat back down. They fell quiet, watching the road. I watched it too.

'If I had a car,' James commented, 'it'd be a Porsche.'

'No – I'd have a Ferrari. Definitely.'

'A Lotus Lamborghini.'

'Yeah. A Lotus. Painted bright red.'

At that moment a white Capri drove past, and Danny was at last able to shout, *'One!'* I knew what Capris looked like, and Princesses, and Minis, but that was about it. I didn't like cars, really. I couldn't see what all the fuss was about – I mean, it would have been different if they could do something special, like fly. That would have been something, then. I pressed against the gate, imagining the scene: what would happen if Mum and Dick Roberts got a car – a yellow car – and it turned out to be magic. There'd be a magic spell, of course, and one day James and I would find out what it was and the car would sprout tiny, feathery wings, and take us off, by ourselves: over the sports field, up into the stars, into all the magic worlds in *The Magic Faraway Tree*–

'They said we were going to get one but we haven't heard anything,' James said.

'What?'

But I knew what he meant. He was talking about social workers again. He slid down off the wall and rested back on his elbows, keeping his eye on the cars.

'*Ten!*' he shouted.

'Yeah, but we hardly ever see Beryl, do we?' Pledgie said. He looked up at Neil, who, still pointedly rubbing his leg, sulkily nodded his assent. 'She's got too many cases to see us much. It will probably be a while before they get round to it.'

Danny and I stayed quiet, watching the road for our colours. I sneaked a look at him out of the corner of my eye. Danny didn't have a social worker. He didn't need one. There was never any trouble for him at home. James and Pledgie teased him about it. They said that he called his mum Mummy and that he still got tucked in to bed and kissed goodnight on the lips. Danny's mum's name was Maureen. She was the only one of our mums who worked. She had a part-time evening job at Securicor, on the phones.

I still remembered the overheard conversation, between the police and Mum. They'd come over again the day they brought James home, and sat in the kitchen for a long time with the adults while James and I waited in the living room. James had smelled bad, and wouldn't speak to me. He'd sat and stared at his feet, and I'd sat next to him on the sofa with my hands in my lap, trying to think of things to say. Then the police came in and spoke to me, and noticed my finger, and asked how I'd managed that, while Nan hovered in the living-room doorway. When they left they said the Social Services would be in touch, but we hadn't heard anything. My finger was all right now, anyway. I didn't have to wear a bandage any more. I was hoping I'd still be wearing it when we went back to school, because then everyone would notice, just like when Leona Thomas, from my old class, fell off the top of the park slide and broke her wrist. People had given her sweets in return for writing on her plaster.

'*Eleven!*'

Pledgie hefted himself up from the wall and knelt on all fours, crawling over to the small strip of grass between our path and the road, and drumming his fists rhythmically against it.

'What are you doing?'

'It gets the worms up. Then we can kill them,' he panted. He banged the ground one more time then straightened, giving up. 'Beryl's all right, really. She takes us out and stuff – buys us milkshakes. My mum says she's nosy. She says they're all nosy, just want to come down here and look down their noses at us.'

A blue Mini rolled by.

'*Eight!*' Pledgie shouted.

If there was a danger list, like Pledgie said, then Pledgie was definitely on it. His family had a bad reputation on the estate. Everyone talked about them. Pledgie told us he'd had quite a few social workers, ever since he was three. He said it was because his mum was on and off the booze, and because his sixteen-year-old brother, Mark, was on drugs. He was a junky, he said. I'd seen him. He looked like an older, thinner version of Pledgie. He was tall, really tall, with an enormous head and sunken eyes, and hair so blond it was almost platinum, cut into a scraggly fringe that barely concealed the pimples and sores covering his forehead. He wore an old black leather jacket and had bad teeth and bad breath, and at night, Pledgie said, he'd leave the house and walk off somewhere – he didn't know where. He didn't go to school or work. He'd already been in prison once, overnight. Pledgie said that it was him that burgled the old people's home, and robbed the number 52 bus-driver with a gun that time. He said the police came round a lot and that Mark had once had some kind of fit, and thrown cans of food and stuff through the front window. One of them had hit his mum in the face and given her a black eye.

'You don't need to worry about Beryl. You just need to know what not to say.'

'Mmm,' James nodded, but without much enthusiasm.

It was getting a bit boring, talking about social workers.

'She's all right, really…'

Pledgie trailed off, trying to think of what else there was.

'What we going to do about the den, then?' James asked, changing the subject. 'Are we going to set one up?'

'We'll need to make a list of all the things we need,' Danny replied.

He pulled his glasses off and rubbed them on his jumper, thinking. Pledgie had asked him if he was a nigger earlier, but Danny had said that only Africans were niggers and his dad was Caribbean, not African, and anyway he was half-half. He hadn't said much for a while, after that.

'Yeah,' James said. 'And we'll need to sort it out so that it's tidy, and waterproof for winter.'

'We can use bin liners for that.'

'And carrier bags. We've got loads at home.'

'We've got an old chair,' Neil joined in. 'Nobody ever sits in it so Shaun and Darren put it up in the attic. I could ask if we can have it. It's a bit saggy, but it's all right.'

'I've got a tin box that locks. We can use that to store things in.'

'What things?' Pledgie said.

He'd been the only one not talking and looked a bit moody. He had been passed over in favour of the den.

'Like...' Danny hesitated.

'We haven't got any things.'

'You know ... den things. Emergency stuff.'

'What do we want to sit around in a muddy shit-hole for, anyway?'

Danny shook his head, shrugged. He put his glasses back on and stared at the road. A red car was driving by, which James hadn't noticed. He was too busy using a stone to chalk his name on the path, in big ungainly capitals. It always worked better when the path was damp, like now. The letters appeared: clumsy, luminous. He nudged Pledgie, who looked down and said, 'So?' but then started to giggle, reluctantly at first, as James wrote F-U-C-K beneath it. James laughed too, and quickly scribbled the word out, so that nobody walking past would see it.

'It'll be good,' he said to Pledgie, about the den, 'as long as we sort it out properly. And we can use Danny's tin to store cigarettes.'

'S'pose,' Pledgie conceded. He took the stone off James, and wrote T-I-T. 'We'd need food, as well.'

'Yeah.'

James took it back, and started writing another word, under T-I-T.

W-A-N-K.

They all giggled.

'Tit wank,' Neil tittered. 'Tit wank. That's when–'

But James reached up and punched him in the leg again, telling him to shut up.

'Ouch! Stop doing that! What do you keep doing that for?'

'Because my nan hears you and I'll be dead.'

'Where will we get the food from?' Pledgie asked. He was getting into it again, his mood forgotten. 'We'll want chocolate, and stuff like that.'

'I get a pound pocket money every week,' Danny offered. 'We can use that.'

We didn't get pocket money.

Pledgie and Neil couldn't have got any either: otherwise they would have said something.

'We could nick some,' Pledgie said.

'What, from home?'

'Yeah, and Deltey's.'

They were stopped from saying more as a door slammed and Stan – Uncle Stan, to us

– walked up his garden path. He was in his work overalls, ready for the night shift. Aunty Barb, his wife, was a dinner lady at my school.

James quickly budged over as he walked towards us, sitting on 'Tit Wank', shielding it from view. They'd been so busy talking he'd forgotten to rub it out.

'Hello, Uncle Stan,' he said.

Uncle Stan said, without stopping, 'Hello, what you two up to? No mischief, I hope.' And he called over his shoulder for us to send his love to that mother of ours; and then he crossed, over to the sports field side of the road. We watched him go.

Neil turned to Pledgie. 'You wouldn't dare,' he said.

'Wouldn't I? How much do you want to bet?'

It was difficult to tell whether Pledgie was joking or not. Neil hesitated. He looked to Danny, but Danny didn't say anything.

'You get into trouble, for nicking stuff.'

Pledgie snorted. 'Yeah, yeah. What's so bad about it, anyway? Everybody else does it.'

James picked up the stone, and started to scribble out the incriminating letters.

'You could get into really bad trouble, for

stuff like that,' Neil repeated.

He looked at James as he said it. James puffed up his cheeks and let out the air in a long, stuttering fart.

'Only if you get caught,' he answered, at last.

His face didn't betray anything. I couldn't tell whether he meant it, or not.

Pledgie grinned and Neil shrugged, giving in.

'S'pose.'

Before they could go any further, there came a sharp rap at the window: it was near sunset, and Nan was calling us in.

33

James wouldn't let me put the light on. I was sure it was because he'd told Pledgie where our bedroom was, and was worried that he'd look up and see that we were already in bed. I was sprawled, belly down, on the bottom bunk, dangling my arm over the mattress ridge. James loitered at the window. He peered out into the dusk, enviously studying the others, who were playing an improvised game of rounders. I could just about see them, too. They were underhand bowling, running over the wet grass, waving a splintered plank of wood in the air. It looked like they were using stones in lieu of their usual tennis ball.

'*Out!*' Pledgie screamed happily.

James turned and kicked the radiator beneath the window in frustration.

'Stop it! You'll get us into trouble!' I whispered, as the sound ricocheted around the room. But he only turned to stick a finger up at me.

I was bored. It wasn't exactly dark, but the evening was dipping into twilight. The room was growing heavy with night particles, which made it too dim to read, while it was still too light for sleep.

My Ken and Barbie were on the floor, by my bed. I picked them up and positioned them, facing each other, on the headboard – as if they were sitting on a bench or fence – and put on my best American voice. 'Do you want to be my girlfriend?' 'Yes, OK.' 'OK. Where shall we go then?' 'Let's go to the cinema and eat popcorn and ice cream.' 'OK, but first you have to give me a kiss.' 'Now?' 'Yes.'

'Shut up, will you?' James snapped,

without looking round.

'Can't make me.'

'Want to bet?'

'Might do.'

I threw Barbie's tiny handbag at him.

It bounced lightly off his head and he half started towards me, before changing his mind.

'Why do I have to share a bedroom with a silly cow like you?' he grumbled.

He kicked the radiator again, to emphasize his point, and this time Nan did shout up the stairs.

'What are you buggers doing up there?'

'Now look what you've done,' I hissed, but James stopped me, putting his fingers to his lips and mouthing, 'Shut up.' We looked at each other, waiting. It was all right. After a second or two she called, 'Get to sleep, or there'll be trouble,' and padded back into the kitchen.

'Silly cow,' James repeated, about Nan this time.

'It's your fault.'

'Shut your face, death-breath.'

'You're the one with the death-breath.'

'Fuck off.'

'F off yourself.'

'What did you say?'

I replied that he had heard me, and after casting one final glance out of the window he came over, snatching Ken and Barbie out of my hands. I made a grab for them but he moved out of reach. He twisted Ken's arm round and punched Barbie in the face, laughing.

'I'll shout for Nan.'

But he knew I wouldn't, not when Dick Roberts was home.

'I'll tell her you've been using the F word.'

'You used it too.'

James sat down on the floor, next to Ken's pink Cadillac. He made a revving noise and laid Barbie on the carpet in front of it, ready to be run over.

'Stupid,' I muttered, looking out of the window, into the sports field. 'I wish I was out there with them, instead of in here with you. They're having lots of fun – you should have a look.'

Actually they were just packing up. I watched as Pledgie tossed the plank of wood away and they filed out of the field, back across the road. As they walked past, I could hear that some sort of argument about who had won was flaring. Pledgie was calling Neil a gyppo, and Neil was telling Pledgie to get stuffed. I glanced over at James to see if he was listening, but he was engrossed. He had abandoned the car, taken Barbie's clothes off, and put Ken's head between her legs.

'Oh, Ken. Don't stop, Ken.'

'You're horrible.'

'Ken, Ken!'

'I mean it. Stop it! You've been mean to me ever since you started hanging round with Pledgie.'

'So? Pledgie's a laugh. Much more than you ever could be.'

He placed Ken and Barbie groin to groin, and made them wriggle around.

'No, he's not,' I said, watching in spite of myself. 'And he's fat and ugly.'

'Look who's talking.'

'I'm not ugly. I'm not fat, either.'

'Yeah, but when you grow pubes you're going to have a ginger minge.'

'I am not.'

I felt a rush of blood to my face, and couldn't think of what else to say. It was one of his new things, calling me ginger, even though he knew my hair was blonde. It was practically the same colour as his. I didn't know what he meant when he talked about 'minge', either. That was one of his and Pledgie's phrases. They giggled whenever they said it. They often said it to each other, over and over again, along with dirty words like 'fuck' and 'cunt' and 'bitches'.

'Nan says it's strawberry blonde,' I said. James only shrugged.

'Nan says it's—'

'Who cares? God, this is so boring.'

'You're the one that's boring.'

'I wish I were still at Pledgie's. We stayed up at night and did what we wanted and I didn't have to listen to you going on and on.'

'Shut up.'

'Shut up yourself, monkey features.'

There was a loud bang outside – someone's exhaust, probably – and James looked round, momentarily distracted. I saw my opportunity and reached over, snatching Barbie out of his hand.

'Hey!' he shouted, as I quickly shoved her out of harm's way, down the wall-side of the bed.

He jumped up and started to scramble over me, but I grabbed his wrist and twisted, as hard as I could.

'Chinese burn!'

'Ouch! Get off!'

He dropped back to the floor, rubbing his arm. There were flashes of white where my fingers had been, the skin around them throbbed an angry red.

'Bitch.'

'So? You shouldn't have taken my Barbie.'

'I wish I were at Pledgie's. It's so boring here.'

He was saying it to get at me. I let out a fart sound, just to show him I didn't care, and climbed under my covers.

'It was brilliant, at Pledgie's.'

'I bet it wasn't. Mum says their house is worse than Aunty Net's.'

'It's not. It's brilliant.'

'And Nan said that Pledgie's mum is never there, and that Pledgie and his brother have to get their own food and stuff.'

'So?'

'So how did you eat, all week? You must have been starving.'

'What's it to you?'

'Nothing.'

'So why are you asking?'

'I already know, anyway.'

And I did already know what he'd done for food. It was how they got found out, at least according to what the police told Mum and Nan. Pledgie's mum had finally worked out that there was a lot of money missing from her handbag (and it was here that Nan said she must have been staying at her boyfriend's for most of the week like everybody knew she did – leaving the kids to fend for themselves – otherwise she'd have noticed much sooner). She'd gone upstairs to Pledgie's room to confront him, and found a) a load of sweet wrappers and b) James, trying to scramble under the bed. She didn't know our family all that well but she knew James by sight and enough about what was going on in the estate to be aware that James was missing.

'I thought you'd run away with the fair,' I said. 'I made up a whole story. I imagined that you were staying with a fortune-teller in a gypsy caravan, and that she didn't have children, and her name was Sharon.'

I remembered the cabin just as I'd imagined it, glowing red in the lamplight, strewn with a multi-coloured, bohemian medley of scarves. One-eyed Sharon, yearning for a son just like James, with her crystals and her false eyeball, which rolled and knocked around in the china mug she kept it in at night, for safekeeping. It seemed silly to think of it now, when really he'd only been around the corner, staying in the boring bedroom of boring Richard Pledge.

'You know that chant we did?'

'What are you going on about?'

'You know what I mean.'

'No.'

I ignored him. I knew he knew what I meant.

'I did another one while you were away. I asked the Killer to bring you back, and it worked.'

'Don't be stupid.'

'It did.'

'I only came back because the police found out. I'd never have, otherwise.'

'It might have been magic, though, that made Pledgie's mum find you,' I said, tracing the patterns of my duvet. It was white, speckled with tiny strawberries.

'Yeah, right.'

I rolled over and looked at him.

'Well? It could have been, you know.'

He had picked up my new Famous Five, and was flicking through it, hardly listening. I noticed again how he was growing more and more – stretching without fattening, like a pre-catapulted elastic band – shooting above me, when earlier in the year he'd only been an inch or so taller.

'I hate it here,' he muttered, petulant. 'I hate you all. I couldn't care less if you all dropped dead.'

'Don't say that.'

'Why not?'

'Because ... you know.'

But he ploughed on, regardless.

'Well, I wouldn't. It would be wicked, I could just go and live with Richard Pledge.'

'Go on then – if that's what you think, why don't you just leave?'

'I might,' he said, and flipped over a couple more pages, before slapping the book shut. He threw it across the floor and started to clamber past me, up the ladder and into his bed. 'I just might.'

'Good,' I replied. I felt briefly tempted, watching his dangling feet disappear, to reach and grab one and yank as hard as I could. 'I couldn't care less if you went to live with Richard Pledge.'

'So?'

'So. So there.'

I rolled over and put my pillow over my head, pulling it off to add, 'I'd have a party if you left.' Then I put it back again, taking care to cover my ears so that I wouldn't be able to hear his reply, because I was sure it would be much worse than anything I could think up. He said something muffled, and I waited for a moment before taking the pillow off.

'Shall I tell you the bride story?'

'No.'

'You know, Nan's ghost story. I'll make it good. Go on, it's your favourite.'

'No.'

'But–'

'What does it take, spack-brain? Are you deaf?'

'Fine. I won't tell it then.' He didn't answer.

Outside somebody walked by, and a dog yelped. It was properly dark by now.

I hesitated, then lifted a finger and prodded the mattress springs above me, feeling at first for where his back was. He couldn't have been asleep, but he didn't stir.

Fine, I thought.

I rolled over and got myself comfortable, pressing my pink cheek against the cool white of the bed-sheet.

Fine.

34

'You're a disgrace, do you hear me?'

It was the peak of visiting hour. There weren't enough chairs to go around again, and James and I were sitting on the floor. I couldn't see their faces, but Nan and Aunty Net were sitting either side of Mum, pitted against each other and they had been arguing ever since we'd arrived over half an hour before and Nan had – or so she said – got a whiff of Aunty Net's breath. Mum lay between them. She looked tired. She'd had something done yesterday morning – the doctors had had 'a bit of a root around', was how Nan'd described it. Anyway, whatever they'd done, it seemed to have taken it out of her. The overhead lights glared and the afternoon sun streamed in through the large, square windows, bleaching her pale face paler still.

Above us, Aunty Net spat impatiently. 'Put a sock in it, you miserable old cow.'

She was giving as good as she got, hardly hesitating before she responded to Nan's asides, but I could see to where her hand dangled, beneath the frame of the bed. A crumpled tissue lay in her lap and she was strumming her fingers, nervously, against the grey plastic of the chair seat. Whenever she stopped strumming, her hand shook.

'Put a sock in it? Put a sock in it? I'll tell you something, my girl – you get off your self-pitying backside and take a look in the mirror. Tell me what you see and then I'll put a sock in it.'

'Here we go. It's like listening to a bloody gramophone.'

'Listening? When have you ever done any listening?'

'I wish you'd listen to yourself,' Aunty Net snapped. She uncrossed and recrossed her legs the other way. 'Then you might realize why I took to the bloody bottle in the first place.'

'Don't you go pointing the finger at me.'

'I'll point my finger wherever I like.'

'Stop it, will you?' Mum pleaded. She rustled, shifting position in bed. 'You're embarrassing me. People are listening.'

I looked around. Nobody seemed to be. A nurse was putting fresh sheets on the opposite bed, which had been emptied, and the old woman in the bed beside that was talking loudly to two equally elderly female friends. The nurses behind the counter were chatting amongst themselves. One of them broke off and reached over to pick up a ringing telephone.

'Keep on and I'll get the nurses to kick you out.'

'Don't you start as well,' Nan grumbled.

But the threat seemed to work, and the argument lulled.

'How's that husband of mine, anyway?'

'The same as ever. Large as life and twice as ugly.'

Dick Roberts wasn't with us. He'd come with Nan and us on Monday and Tuesday, but Nan had gone up to the hospital early yesterday, while he was still at work, and he was on overtime today.

'Is he getting enough sleep?'

'How the bloody hell should I know?'

'You know he's a bad sleeper.'

'Yes, and? What do you expect me to do – go in at night and check?'

'You never know, Mum. She might have been hoping you'd offered your services, then she wouldn't have to bother.'

'You what? If you haven't got anything nice to say keep your filthy mouth shut.'

They started up again. James sat beside me, his blond hair flopping over his forehead as he raced his matchbox car around the bed and chair legs. He made a soft screeching noise, skidding the car over the tiles, before crashing it into my thigh. I wriggled away, shooting him a dirty look. He giggled as he reversed the car, and took it off in another direction.

'Sometimes I find it hard to believe that you're my own flesh and blood,' Nan snapped, above me.

She stretched a leg, knocking her shoe against my knee, and I turned to see that her tea-coloured tights were wrinkled ever so slightly against her shoes. She had brushed clear nail-varnish over a small ladder, which had formed on her left ankle. Poorly disguised blue and purple veins snaked and intertwined beneath the nylon, tangling like ivy-vines, creeping symptoms of old age. There was a faint hint of fabric conditioner and tumble dryer about her; she smelled comforting, warm.

'That makes two of us, then, doesn't it?'

'Will you shut up? Shut up or go home, the both of you. I didn't come into hospital to sit and listen to you two arguing.'

'Well—'

'I mean it. One more word out of you two and I'll call the sister over. What are you smirking at, Net? Do you think I'm joking?'

Aunty Net pushed her chair back. Her handbag swung off the ground.

'I'm going to the loo,' she said.

She tick-tacked past us, her footsteps ringing clear against the hard floor.

'Does she think I was born yesterday?' Nan muttered, turning to watch her go.

'Give it a rest, Mum. You know she's

having a bad week.'

Nan grunted in response and shifted in her chair again, picking up her handbag and fishing around in it until she brought out a half-eaten pack of soft mints.

'She's not getting any sympathy from me, if that's what you're asking.'

'You're too hard on her.'

'Too hard on her? For Christ's sake, Katherine, she should be thankful that I'm still bloody talking to her,' Nan said, popping a sweet into her mouth and turning to look down at us.

'S'pose you two want one now, don't you?' she said, passing the packet to me.

I passed it on to James, who took two.

'I saw that, greedy guts.'

'So? I'm hungry,' James complained. He jumped up, walking around the bed to the window and rolling his car up and down on the sill. 'When are we going to go home and have some tea?'

'We're visiting your mother. Where are your manners?'

Nan shot him an evil look and started to say more, about how he'd been a pain in the neck ever since the holidays, but Mum cut her short.

'Take him to the café, would you? Get him

a sandwich, or a packet of crisps.'

'He can learn to wait.'

'No, go on. My purse is in the drawer.'

She struggled in bed, reaching over to the cabinet, but Nan waved her away and told her not to worry, they'd sort it out later.

'Come on then, you greedy bugger,' she said to James.

She stood up, giving her skirt a quick brush, and they disappeared around the corner, in the same direction as Aunty Net.

'Get something for Janny too,' Mum called after them.

I bit down on my sweet, feeling the crisp surface shatter and crack. Warm menthol and sugar-flavoured spit swam around my gums. On the other side of the room the old women put on their coats and said something to their friend about having to get back, what with it being bingo night. They said they'd buy a line or two for her, too, and let her know if she won anything.

'Janny?' Mum said, from the bed. 'Yes?'

I ran a finger over the polished floor, bored.

'Come on, get up. Let me have a look at you ... that's better. You all right, then?'

I shrugged and nodded, wondering what

she wanted to have a look at me for, when she got to have a look at me every single day.

'Your dad all right? Not been too bad, has he?'

She didn't seem to expect an answer. I almost sat back down again but as she was still watching me I thought better of it and, folding my hands behind my back, began to step slowly around the rim of her bed. I could fit two footsteps to each tile if I was careful to put one foot directly in front of the other, toe to heel.

'What you up to?'

'Walking.'

'That's all right, then.'

The checks spread over the floor, like an enormous chessboard: white, black, white, black.

'Don't step on the cracks, or the monster will get you.'

I nodded. The last of the mint syrup swirled in my mouth. I licked my gums, savouring it.

Mum coughed, softly. 'Where's Annette got to?' she murmured, glancing over to the corridor.

The tea lady came in at that moment. She wheeled her trolley over, the cups and saucers jiggling noisily. She was wearing the same type of chequered blue pinafore that Nan often wore, and her black hair was pulled back into a tight bun. Her little black eyes looked just like currants. She asked Mum in a thick foreign accent which she wanted: tea or coffee. Mum shook her head, declining either. She watched the woman leave and switched her attention back to me.

'Come here. You've got a bit of muck on your face.'

I obediently climbed up onto the side of the bed. She held onto my arm, breathing heavily, and licked her fingers. 'There, that's better...'

'Do me a favour, will you, later?' she said, as she turned my face right and left, to check if there was anything else. There wasn't, and she contented herself with giving my cheek a final rub. 'Pop over to your aunty's for me later, make her a cup of tea. Can you do that?' I nodded.

'Do it before it gets dark, though.'

'All right.'

She smiled and let go of my arm, saying, 'Good girl.'

'Shall I get down?'

'No, it's all right – might as well stay here, eh, now you're up?' she said, and patted a space right next to her. 'What are you

286

waiting for? Come on, I won't bite.'

I nudged over until I was sitting with her, up against the pillow.

'There,' she said, resting a hand on my shoulder. 'That's not so bad, is it?'

We sat, quietly. There was a good view from the window. I watched as two cars and an ambulance drove round the hospital roundabout and into the suburban streets, beyond. The late afternoon sun glinted, bright against the red brick of the chimneys.

'It's getting a bit long, isn't it?' she murmured. She meant my hair. She started to stroke it, ploughing her fingers deep into the curls. 'I'll have to take you up to Jimmy's next week.'

My tummy rumbled. Mum talked on. I could feel her lips, tickling the top of my head.

'You're a good girl.'

Across the room, the old lady – her friends gone – coughed, and lay back in bed. She looked over as she did and smiled, and Mum brought her free hand up to give a little wave. Her nametag slid up her wrist, just like a bangle. Katherine Jane Bainbridge, it read, in neat blue biro capitals, 17.03.1948.

'Such a good girl,' Mum repeated.

She pressed her lips down onto my crown,

giving me a small kiss. I leaned back, nestling in the crook of her arm. I hoped Nan would remember that I didn't like cheese and onion crisps. Mum's belly was soft against my back. I could feel her breathing, coarse and deep.

35

There wasn't any milk in the house but Aunty Net didn't seem to mind.

She sat, sipping from the chipped mug. Her two hands were clenched tightly around it, as though she needed the warmth.

'I've got to sort myself out,' she muttered, more to herself than to me.

She took another sip.

'Trouble is...' she started, and then stopped, looking out of the sitting-room window, at the overgrown jungle of grass and weeds out the back. 'I never saw him starting over, did I? I always saw him in some London gutter.'

I nodded in agreement, even though I wasn't quite sure who she was actually talking about. Uncle Peter, her second husband, I guessed.

'He deserved to be in the gutter. Turned me into this, he did,' she spat, jabbing a finger into her chest. 'Ruined my life.'

'I better go, Aunty Net. Nan said I could only stay for half an hour.'

'He could have come back,' she finished, sadly, 'and started over with me.'

I stood up, and said again that I'd better get a move on. She finally took notice, and reached out to touch my arm.

'Don't go just yet. Stay for a few more minutes.'

'I can't...'

'Tell you what, I'll show you something.'

She stood up and hurried across the room, bending down to pick up a square tin, which lay on the carpet, by the television.

'Look,' she said. She brought it over and sat back down on the sofa, almost squashing Manilow, who spat and swiped at her before burying his face into his paws and drifting back into sleep. 'I rooted this out, yesterday. It was in one of the upstairs cupboards.'

It was a Fox's biscuit tin, the type Mum always bought from the Sainsbury's in Cowley Centre, for Christmas. Only this one was old. The veneer was marbled and chipping off – almost as if a mouse, attracted by the lingering scent and mistaking them for the real, had been trying to nibble at the illustrated biscuits: Jammy Dodgers, chocolate digestives, pink wafer sandwiches. Aunty Net prised open the lid, and shook the contents over the carpet, in front of us.

'Tons of them,' she murmured.

And she began to turn them over, square upon square of family photographs: both older and newer, colour and black and white, a motley crew of borders and sizes, a jumble of smiling faces. They looked mismatched: like a collection of different jigsaw puzzle pieces, which had lost their rightful place and had come to rest together through accident rather than design.

'I'd almost forgotten I had them.'

There were shots of Nan and Mum and us, of Uncle Terry and even a couple of Dick Roberts, but mainly they were of Aunty Net's own family: Uncle Lenny, Uncle Peter, Jason and Valerie, in school uniform and in casual clothes, playing at the seaside, at a birthday party, unwrapping presents next to a Christmas tree as Aunty Net, orange Christmas cracker crown atop her head, leaned over the sofa – the sofa we were sitting on now – watching.

'Look at this,' Aunty Net said, picking one up and passing it to me.

It was a posed photo, professional, at a zoo. Aunty Net stood, young in a pink summer dress. A breeze was blowing her black curls into her face. She was clutching Valerie's legs around her shoulders, and Valerie's head popped up, over Aunty Net's. A spider monkey perched – nonchalant, gripping a peanut – on top of her own dark, frizzy locks. It must have been a hot day; the photo had that bleached look of too much sun, and both Aunty Net and Valerie were squinting. They were smiling though, as well, really smiling.

'There's one of Jason like that somewhere too, with Pete.'

She peered over my shoulder, looking at the photo one last time before she took it back, and dropped it onto the floor.

'My little girl, she was. It doesn't seem like yesterday, when we took that ... but look at me now. Two kids down, an old boozer, and on my second divorce.'

'Look at this place,' she murmured.

She wrinkled her nose and pulled her cardigan tightly around her middle, looking around.

'I better get a move on,' I said. I thought she was going to ignore me again, but she didn't.

'Go on then,' she replied, and managed a small smile, which quickly drooped and died. 'Where's that brother of yours, anyway? Shouldn't you be with him?'

'He's playing with his friends.'

But she'd already stopped listening. She was leaning down, trailing her fingers over the layers of faces. I tried not to notice the large tear trickling down her cheek, and turned away.

'Thanks for the tea, sweetheart,' I heard her call, before I closed the door.

36

James and Pledgie were playing Kerbie on the intersection of Hazelnut Path and Cumberland Road, the narrow strip that divided Aunty Net's block of houses from ours. James stood on the side nearest our house, waiting for Pledgie's throw.

'Come on,' he complained.

Pledgie ignored him. He tried to balance the football on one of his fingers and spin it round, like they did in basketball, but the ball only toppled out of his hands and bounced into the road, coming to a stop beneath a parked car. James ran to get it, grumbling to himself.

'Spack-brain. I'm not playing any more, this is boring.'

I crossed over and sat down next to Neil and Danny on the pavement. They were flicking through Danny's football sticker album. Different players stared out from the pages, in single portraits and group photos. Neil's face showing flashes of animation as he called out the names of the footballers he recognized. He was wearing an old green T-shirt. It was too big for him; it hung over his diminutive frame and ended halfway down his thighs, like a mini-dress. There was a smear of mud over his cheek, and his profile – with his nose and mousy hair – made him look like a beaky, baby sparrow. James came over and sat down on the other side of Danny. He lodged the football between his legs and flicked his hair out of his eyes, leaning over to take a look at the stickers.

'It's my ball, moron, give it me,' Pledgie whined, slumping down next to him.

He tried to thump the ball free of James's legs, bringing his fists down hard on the top. James pushed him away. Seeing that he wasn't getting anywhere, Pledgie turned to

Danny, and punched him on the back. Danny looked up, colouring.

'What was that for?'

'Because I felt like it.'

'Well, don't.'

'Why? What you going to do about it?'

'Get stuffed.'

'Don't tell *me* to get stuffed,' Pledgie shouted. He clambered up from the kerb and started to wrestle Danny, from behind. Danny flailed helplessly, and it was easy work for Pledgie – who was the bigger of the two – to get him into a headlock, and snatch the album away.

'Don't!'

'Try and stop me.'

He held the album out of reach, imitating Danny as he blinkingly fumbled for his glasses, which had fallen off in the tussle. Finding them at last, Danny thrust them back in place and grabbed the album. Pledgie backed away, holding fast. There was a tearing sound as he did, and one of the pages ripped.

'Look, James, look at his face! He's going to cry.'

'I'm not.'

James looked round and snickered obligingly, saying, 'Pussy' to Danny. Pledgie looked pleased. He threw the album out into the road.

'You can always Sellotape it,' I offered, as Danny sat down next to me. He nodded and examined the damage, fingering the tear. His cheeks were still flushed from Pledgie's throttling, and he was breathing heavily. I felt sorry for him.

'I'm bored,' Pledgie moaned. 'Let's go to the den, or something.'

'I can't tonight. My mum said I've got to go home early, she says I'm never in.'

'I wasn't asking you, Gyppo. What about you, Jamie boy?'

'Nah.'

'Why? Because your nan won't let you?'

'No.' James reddened. He picked up a stone and started to tap it over the pavement, leaving a trail of tiny white marks. 'Don't be stupid. I can do what I want. We should just leave it until we've got the stuff for it, tomorrow.'

'What stuff?' I asked.

'There's not much point until then, is there? There won't be anything to do.'

Pledgie shrugged. 'S'pose so,' he said. 'What shall we get, anyway?'

'Well ... it's like we said, isn't it?' James said. He dropped the stone and leaned back on his elbows, looking pleased. He liked it when they asked him what to do. 'Neil, you got to ask for that chair from your attic, and Danny, you're bringing that tin you've got, right?'

Danny nodded. 'Yeah.'

'And then there's just the stuff for it – like we agreed. Let's get a couple of bars at first. A bar each, just to see if we can.'

'What bars?' I asked. 'Bars of what?'

James glanced round at me, irritated.

'Shut your face, will you?'

The others were looking. I flushed and shut up, looking down at my shoes. The toes were already a bit scuffed; the black veneer had rubbed off to reveal the dull grey beneath. They were practically new, we'd gone and got them just before school started. Mum would kill me when she saw them. She said James and I would bankrupt her, the way that we got through them.

'Are you really going to do it?' Danny asked, breaking the quiet.

He took his glasses off and inspected them. His cheeks had calmed down, but he'd taken the precaution of sitting on his album, so nobody else could take it.

'You've scratched them,' he mumbled, spitting onto his sleeve and wiping one of the frames.

'What do you mean, are we really going to do it? You chickening out already?'

'No. I just didn't think you were serious. That's all.'

'I'm going to do it,' Neil said, hurriedly. 'I'm no chicken.'

He looked round at Pledgie and James, for confirmation.

'Yeah, see,' Pledgie said. He slung his arm casually around Neil's shoulder, and started to make clucking noises at Danny. 'Chick-chick-chick-en.'

'Shut up.'

'Chick-chick–'

'Shut up!'

'Going to make me?'

'I'm going home, anyway.'

'What are you–' I started one more time, but James prodded me in the ribs, cutting me off. I made a spastic face at him, and carried on. 'Tell me. Bars of what?'

'Bars of what?' he mimicked. 'Bars of what? Bars of what? Bars of what?'

'Shut up.'

'Shut up. Shut up. Shut up.'

The others laughed, even Danny, who must have been relieved that they were having a go at someone else. I pulled a sulky face and said that I'd tell Nan, but it didn't seem to matter, and they all started to tease me, chanting, 'I'll tell Nan, I'll tell Nan, I'll tell Nan', and then 'Shut up, shut up, shut up' and 'Get lost, get lost, get lost', right up until Nan appeared at the garden gate, looking cross, in her dressing gown. She asked the others whether they didn't have any homes to go to, and they quickly disappeared.

'I told you not to hang around with that Richard Pledge,' Nan scolded James.

James made a face and carried on eating his bowl of Rice Krispies. Nan had let us have a bowl each before we went up to bed, and we were sitting at the kitchen table. She stood by the window, her arms folded. The pink rollers in her fringe stood out in contrast to the grey tint of her skin.

'Don't you look at me like that,' she said. She took a fag from her packet, which was on the sideboard, and lit up. 'What did I tell you, about hanging round with that Pledge boy? Eh? Do you think I was joking? Do you think I said it for the sake of my health?'

'Mum didn't say I couldn't.'

'That's because your mother doesn't know. Anyway, that's enough of your cheek,' she said, pausing to take a long drag. 'You do as you're told. She's home tomorrow and I don't want any upsets.'

Dick Roberts entered the kitchen at that moment, holding an empty mug. Nan raised her eyebrows, and fell silent. She picked up an ashtray from the side and, tapping her ash into it, leaned back against the draining board, eyeing him with ill-concealed irritation. Dick Roberts didn't look at her, or say anything. He switched the kettle on and set about making himself a cup of tea, banging cupboard doors open and shut, leaving a trail of white grains as he slopped the sugar bowl down onto the counter.

I carried on eating my cereal. It had been in the milk too long and was starting to lose its crunch. There was a sudden movement outside as a cat jumped up onto our wall. Nan saw it. She pulled up the nets, banging on the window.

'Shoo!'

Dick Roberts finished. He dropped the teabag and teaspoon into the sink, on his way out. I listened as the living-room door pulled open and shut, and looked over at Nan, who had turned and was staring at the puddle of water and milk he'd left behind.

'That's right,' she muttered to herself. 'Just leave it there.'

She stubbed out the remnants of her cigarette and reached for her packet again, plucking out a fresh one. I watched her and noticed, for the first time, how tired she looked. Really worn out. She fumbled with her lighter, and glanced up, catching my eye.

'What are you gawping at?' she snapped, pulling the cigarette out of her mouth. 'I've had a bellyful of you two today. Get upstairs, out of my sight.'

37

'Do you ever wonder why the sky's blue? Mrs Foster says it's a reflection of water, but there's only the stream around here ... and that's brown.'

James didn't bother to look round.

'Anyway, the stream's not big enough for our bit of sky.'

I dragged my bag and wandered along behind him, tripping over the concrete, feeling the bag bounce and hop in time with my footsteps. There was a nip in the morning air and the sky wasn't blue at all, it was a dreary grey. The road was clogged with my schoolmates. They walked slowly by, shouting and chattering, swinging their packed-lunch boxes through the air. We'd left the house early, so that James had time to get to school, but there were already a few scattered groups in the playground.

James stopped.

'You just said hurry up.'

'Shut up,' he said, plucking a felt-tip pen out of his pocket.

He crouched down, and began to scrawl on the sports field railings: *James woz ere.* I watched him, knocking my heel impatiently against the ground. He carried on writing, holding the lid between his teeth: *James R is cool.* The black of the felt-tip stood out against the yellowing white, and tiny flakes of the bubbly paint broke off with the pressure of the nib.

'You'll get caught, you know.'

He used his spare hand to flip the v-sign at me.

'Who asked you?'

Janet R is a Flid. IDT. INDT.

'You'll get into trouble if they catch you.'

'Fuck off, Flid.'

But he stopped, nonetheless, and put his pen back in his pocket. I waited, watching as he stood up and, slinging his bag over his shoulder, crossed the road.

'I'm not picking you up from school later,' he called, as he left.

'I'll tell Nan if you don't!'

'You do, and you're dead.'

Mrs Foster was off sick that day. I didn't know what with. Mr Archer filled in for the morning period. He was the deputy head, and he didn't stand any nonsense. The hours with him dragged by in restless silence. I'd thought we were getting him for the rest of the day but then, as the lunch bell rang, he made us sit still in our seats while he had a final word. That was what he'd called it: 'I'd like a final word with you lot.' And then he put on his low, slow, forbidding tone, the one that nobody dared quarrel with.

'Now,' he started. 'Now ... I'm sure you'll be very sorry to hear that I'm in a meeting this afternoon. It's not something I can get out of. Otherwise, of course, I'd gladly continue to teach you myself. However ... however, seeing as I'm unable to reschedule – Miss Brennan, what does reschedule mean? It means rearrange – seeing as I'm unable to reschedule, Mrs Turbot has very kindly agreed to come in and take you for the afternoon period. Do you remember Mrs Turbot? You do? Good.'

At this stage he broke off and, unsmiling, let his eyes wander over the class, from face to face, hovering slightly longer on the troublemakers. He hardly looked at me but I still blushed and stared down at my desk, squirming.

'Now, I think it goes without saying that I'm expecting you to treat Mrs Turbot with just as much respect as you have treated me this morning. If I do hear that there's been any – *any* – trouble, just remember that it will be me you have to deal with. Have I made myself clear?'

A few of us nodded meekly.

'I said, have I made myself clear?'

'Yes, Mr Archer.'

'Excellent,' he said. He clapped his hands together and allowed a short, thin-lipped smile. 'That's exactly what I wanted to hear. Off you go.'

Of course, it didn't mean a thing. He must have known that. We'd had Mrs Turbot before: she was known around the school as a soft touch. Whenever she came it was like having a holiday in school hours. By the time the afternoon bell rang and we filed in from lunch break – to form an impatient line outside the classroom door – the atmosphere was totally different. The deferential quiet had disappeared: people were talking, chewing, using their biros to scribble on the wall; a couple of scuffles had broken out. There was a cheer as Mrs Turbot walked down the corridor register pressed to her chest, and everybody ignored her pseudo-stern stares.

Now, there she was, an hour and a half later, having abandoned her latest attempt at installing some order. She sat there, slumped at Mrs. Foster's desk, in front of the black-board – which was bare aside from the large white capitals declaring 'SILENCE IN CLASS' – and watched, helpless, as we roared and screamed. I felt sorry for her but there wasn't anything I could do.

I wriggled, and glanced half-heartedly down at my copy of *Charlotte's Web*, which was open on the desk in front of me, before turning in my seat to gaze out of the window. Outside, the initially grey day had turned clear and mild. The estate was softened and warmed by the yellow sun and the mellow reds of the few trees I could see. Our classroom was on the first floor of the double-stacked, prefabricated school building, and offered a good view. Below me, on Cumberland Road, a bus drove past the school railings. I wondered whether Mum and Nan were on it. Nan had said this morning that Mum would be back by the time we got home. I'd asked her whether they'd come in an ambulance, but she had only replied that she was in no mood for silly questions. 'Anyway, what do we need an ambulance for?' she'd snapped. 'Listen to yourself, you'll be packing us away in coffins next.' But how was I to know? It wasn't as if she – or Mum – had ever taken the time to tell us what was actually wrong.

I could just about see Wesley Green Middle School from where I was sitting: across the sports field and over Cuddeston Way, where tiny cars were driving to and fro. There was movement in the playground. Games, I supposed. I wondered whether James was out there – and Danny, Neil and Pledge. I wondered what they were up to, whether they were playing football, or busy whispering in class, and planning the logistics of their den.

'Janet?'

I looked up. A paper ball whizzed over my head. Across the class one of the boys let out a loud burp, which was followed by an appreciative ripple of laughter. Mrs Turbot was standing over me. Her short brown bob flopped over her middle-aged, wary face; she was frowning.

'I want you to take this to Mr Archer's office,' she said, holding out a folded note.

I blushed. A brief hush fell as the others turned, to watch. It wasn't hard to guess what she must have written, and there was a wave of complaint: 'Oh, miss, don't do that, miss', 'We promise we'll be quiet, miss', 'Please, miss.'

Mrs Turbot ignored them.

'If he's not there, take it to Mrs Broad's.'

Mrs Broad was the headmistress. If you called her Miss instead of Mrs she made you stay in at break.

'Be quick.'

There wasn't anything I could do. I closed my book, put it away in my desk drawer and stood up.

'Yes, miss,' I said, as quietly as I could. Then I took the note, and left.

38

They were at the school gates. I knew immediately that they were waiting for me. Five of them from my class: three girls and two boys. Sasha Brennan and the twins, Tanya and Tracey Best. They stood whispering now, the two of them, their mouths conspiratorial beneath black and brunette bobs. A single duplicated face glared out at me, from beneath each fringe. The boys – Derek Wayne and Christopher Clerkin – stood, slouching against the railings with boyish affectation, watching me and nudging each other with their elbows.

I swallowed and hovered, looking hopefully around for James. There was no sign of him, of course; I hadn't thought there would be. There were just other schoolchildren, pushing through the main doors past me, skipping, playing, having a quick game of hopscotch or footy before home. Barney was the only adult in sight, and he was busy with the road. There wasn't anybody to stop a fight.

For a second or two, I thought about going in to find Mr Archer and telling him, even though I knew it would create more trouble. I quickly changed my mind: I couldn't dob anyone in, James would never forgive me.

Anyway, I thought, it would be better to go home now – while there were still people around.

I clutched my school bag to my chest and took a deep breath. I probably wouldn't have managed it, even then, if I hadn't suddenly remembered Pledgie's taunts from last night, the way he had clucked 'Chicken, chick-chick-chicken' at Danny. I pictured him doing it to me and, with a flush of indignation, hurried up the path, past them.

They picked up their bags and followed, a few paces behind.

Don't panic, I told myself. The school railings flicked along, flashing green strips on the edge of my vision. I kept going, past the playground, past the fairies' tree trunks and the giant's hill.

Thirty, thirty-one, thirty-two, I muttered softly, counting my steps.

I was doing well, over thirty already.

And it couldn't be many steps to home.

It was only five minutes from school, if that.

Then, once we were out of Barney's sight, they started taunting me.

Softly at first, then louder and louder.

'Teacher's pet.'

'We're going to get you.'

'Spammy Janet.'

That stupid Mrs Turbot, I thought angrily. Why did she have to go and ask me?

'I'll set my brother on you,' I shouted hurriedly over my shoulder at them, as I stepped down from the pavement and crossed the intersection of Crowberry Road.

Seventy-six, seventy-seven...

Then: the first push in the back. It wasn't hard but it was enough. I swallowed once, twice, and tried to ignore the funny churning in my stomach. Come on, I thought – there wasn't far to go, a little way more and I'd cross Hazelnut Path and be home.

'He'll get you – you just wait – I swear.'

You're almost there, I told myself, and stepped up another gear. Almost there. I tripped slightly in my hurry and they laughed, but I didn't look around, or say anything more. The back of my knees felt funny, like they might buckle any minute. I could almost see home. It was just a few more steps. Another hundred and I'd be at the gate. They wouldn't dare touch me, then.

'Where is he then, Spamet? Come on then, where's your brother?'

'Yeah.'

One hundred and ten, eleven, twelve…

One of them broke away, rushing forward to pull up the back of my skirt.

'Ergh! Did you see that?'

'Skanky pants!'

'Skiddy britches!'

One hundred and twenty-three, twenty-four, twenty-five… I walked faster and faster, stopping just short of a trot – twenty-six, twenty-seven – trying to ignore the knocking in my chest. First years loitered ahead of me, blocking the path as they gossiped and bickered, slowing my way. I looked around quickly, saw that there were no cars and bolted across the road. The gang followed. A stone whizzed past my legs, clattering onto the far kerb.

Twenty-eight, twenty-nine, thirty…

I crossed back over.

I could see home now, a tiny sliver of brick peeking out of the jut of the garages.

Another push in the back.

I stumbled, but kept going.

Forty, forty-one…

And another, harder.

Forty-two…

And another. It was six pairs of hands this time rather than one and I fell, dropping my bag and grazing my knees on the gravelly pavement. I gritted my teeth, held back tears and started to pick myself up, but they had surrounded me by then. One of the boys grabbed hold of me and pinned my arms around my back.

'Go on, get her.'

There was a cheer as Tanya Best grabbed my bag. She opened it and scattered the contents over the ground. Pens and pencils, a ruler and my exercise books clattered out. My collection of marbles cascaded down the dirty slant of the pavement, tumbling onto the road. Out of the corner of my eye I saw the tiny turquoise one, my favourite, slide down a drain. It disappeared with a dull plop. A foot appeared from behind me, stamping down on a pencil. The wood buckled and cracked, the red lead broke. Someone yanked my ponytail, jerking my neck backwards.

'She's crying!' Tracey shouted, jubilant.

'Pull her knickers down!'

'I bet they've got skids in!'

There was a whoop and they bent down, yanking my pleats over my shirt. I started to struggle– 'Stop it! Stop!' – but it was six against one. A hand tugged on the rim of my pants and pulled them down to my knees.

'Look at her! Baldy! Bald minge!'

'Skiddy knickers!'

'Get off! GET OFF!'

The voice was vaguely familiar. I stood, shaking, as a raw, wild-faced woman pushed in, leaning forward to grab my arms. She was haggard with illness, with vivid skin and red veins running like lace over her cheeks. The confusion lasted for less than an instant, and I realized it was Aunty Net.

She dropped her bags to the floor with an angry bang – two of them: her handbag and a white plastic carrier bag, which fell with the sharp knock of glass and swish of upset liquid. She broke up the circle, swearing incoherently, flailing her arms and knocking the kids, who weren't much smaller than she was, out of the way. The group scattered, realigning at a safe distance.

'Go on. Piss off.' She was calmer now, but there was still an edge to her voice, a no-messing, furious force that made up for her diminutive stature.

I stood, wiping my eyes with the back of my hand, feeling the cold snot coating the top of my lips.

'Fucking little brats. How could you?

What's she ever done to you? Go on, piss off.'

'Why should we?'

'Yeah, why should we?'

'Piss off, I said. Fuck off, the lot of you ... ganging up like that. It's disgusting.'

She knelt down, muttering soothing words at me as she hastily wiped my face and wrenched my knickers back into place. Her face was livid – part alcohol, part anger – and her eyes were twinkling savagely. Her breath was hot and potent.

'Come on, darling. Why didn't you run to mine? It's only over there, you silly bugger. Come on, anyway, pick your things up.'

And then, over at them, angry again: 'You wait until later, you vicious sods. I'm coming round your houses, do you hear me? I know where you live. I'll see what your parents have to say about this.'

'Yeah, yeah.'

'You do and my mum'll kick your face in.'

But the threat worked. She was an adult, after all, and it might just have been true that she knew where they lived. They disbanded, casting shouts and aspersions over their shoulders as they disappeared.

'Little bastards,' Aunty Net muttered. 'You all right, darling? You got everything?

Come on, let's get you home.'

I hesitated. She looked down at me and I looked again at her bloodshot eyes and chapped smile. I understood Nan's censorious anger for the first time. It wasn't just a game, there was more to it than their routine bickering. She was right, Aunty Net was killing herself. But Aunty Net was right as well. It was misery, not her, that was doing it.

'You all right?' she repeated. Her sad eyes sparkled kindly.

I nodded and tried out a small smile, giving my cheeks a final wipe.

'Good. That's what I like to hear. Let's get those knees of yours cleaned up, shall we?'

She stood up, grunting with the struggle, holding a hand to her thigh for balance. She picked up her handbag and the plastic bag she had dropped, and I took hold of the hand she proffered.

'There we are ... soon be home ... you OK?'

'Yes,' I said.

I looked up, flashing her another weak smile, and noticed that she'd stopped listening. She was looking over at our house, where a police car had just drawn up to the kerb.

'What the–?' she muttered.

Her grip on my hand tightened.

A policeman got out of the car. He opened the rear door and, after a second or two, just as the first spots of rain began to fall, a small blond head emerged.

'For fuck's sake,' Aunty Net said. She broke into a trot, pulling me along with her. 'It never rains but it bloody pours. What's that little shit been up to now?'

39

'How could you?' Nan hissed as she came back into the kitchen, after letting the policeman out. She walked over to the window, where the rain was still falling lightly against the pane, blurring the glass and leaving the landscape an indiscriminate smudge of grey and green. 'The very day your mother gets home, and you go and do this?'

Mum was sat at the kitchen table, her chin propped in her hands, her eyes closed. She was still in her coat. Her suitcase was at her feet. James sat at the table, opposite her, avoiding eye contact with anyone. A semblance of his usual defiance hovered in

315

the cocky jut of his chin, but I could see a faint movement, where he was biting at his inner lip. I stood in the doorway, with Aunty Net's hands resting on my shoulders, watching them. My knees were stinging, but somehow it didn't feel like the time to bring it up.

'I don't know – kids,' Aunty Net offered, but neither Mum nor Nan took any notice.

'Haven't you got any common sense?' Nan spat at James. She started to take her headscarf off, yanking the knot apart. Beside her the kettle gargled noisily, and a thread of steam wound upwards, coating the overhead cupboard with a thin sheet of condensation. 'What about your father? What do you think he's going to say?'

James shrugged. Nan watched him, her lips twisting.

'Go on, what's he going to do when you tell him you've been stealing? Let me tell you, my boy – he's going to thump you all the way to hell and back.'

She dropped her scarf on the sideboard and opened the overhead cupboard, pulling two mugs out.

'He's going to knock the living daylights out of you, and for the first time in my life I can't say that I blame him.'

She brought the sugar bowl down with an extra hard bang and started to say something more, but Mum was seized by a sudden fit of coughing. Nan broke off, looking round. She watched for a moment or two, as Mum doubled over the table, before she ripped off a square of kitchen roll and walked over.

'Come on, Katie Jane,' she said, with a sigh.

She held the tissue to Mum's mouth and waited, with her hand on Mum's back. Nobody spoke. After a few moments the phlegmatic hacking began to trail off, and Mum looked up.

'All right?'

Mum nodded. She sat, dabbing at her lips with the sodden tissue. Her eyes were watering, and two clownish black rivers ran down her flushed cheeks.

'You sure?' Nan asked. She hovered over her for a second or two more, just to be certain, and then turned, giving James another filthy look. 'I hope you're happy now, you little swine.'

James shrugged again, though I noticed he still avoided her eyes. Nan's face darkened. She put her hands on her hips, and it looked as though she was about to launch back into her tirade, but at that moment the garden gate whined. It was Dick Roberts, walking up the drive.

Nan glanced at Mum.

The front door slammed.

'Don't tell him,' Mum said. Her voice was low and hoarse; she was still wheezing slightly. She stifled a small cough, and looked at Nan pleadingly. 'Don't tell him, I don't want a scene. Please?'

'You can't let him get away with it, Katie.'

It was too late, anyway. Dick Roberts pushed past me and Aunty Net, into the kitchen. He was carrying a bunch of red carnations, and his blue overalls and face were covered in a fine down of rain. He dropped his holdall and looked from Nan to Mum, running a hand through his wet hair.

'Don't tell me what?'

He began to move at the mention of *stealing*. I shot across the room and backed into the sink as Dick Roberts wrenched James up by the fringe of his hair and pulled him into the middle of the floor. James let out a low wail, and shielded his face with his hands. Aunty Net and Nan sprang forward. Aunty Net grabbed hold of Dick's arm, but Dick Roberts used his free hand and pushed her away. She staggered backwards but didn't fall.

'Dick!' Mum cried. *'Dick, no!'*

She went to get up from her chair but sank back into it, either too exhausted or too horrified.

Other voices rose from the tangle of bodies.

'I'll break his fucking neck!'

'That's enough!'

'Get off him!'

Aunty Net fell back against the sideboard one, two times. Feet collided with each other, limbs merged. It was all noise and confusion. I put my fingers in my ears and shut my eyes. There was a thud – someone falling – and it was only a few seconds later, when I dared to open them again, that I saw it had stopped. James was slumped against a cupboard door, his feet curled beneath him as he sniffed loudly and wiped the tears from his face. He'd fallen over Aunty Net's bags and the vodka bottle had tumbled over the floor, towards me. Aunty Net stood slightly to one side, by the kitchen door, with one hand to her chest, recovering her breath. A long, dark thread of hair was sticking to her cheek.

'Dick?'

It was Mum. I looked over at her. She was watching Dick Roberts, who was in turn looking down at Nan. Nan stood, steadily facing the hand that he had raised, against her.

'Come on, love – stop that,' Mum pleaded, but he didn't seem to hear her.

'I'm sick of you,' Dick Roberts stammered. 'Always interfering ... just because you've got Katie under the thumb you think...'

'Go on then,' Nan said. She tapped the corner of her forehead.

Neither of them moved. Nan stood, quite still. Dick Roberts stared down at her, blinking rapidly. A pulse throbbed at the corner of his jaw. His lips twitched.

'I will, you know. I – I will.'

'What are you waiting for? I haven't got all day.'

But he couldn't do it, after all. He took a step backwards, and dropped his hand to his side. Nan watched him for a moment or two, taking in the lowered head and downcast eyes. And then she started to turn away.

'You Robertses,' she muttered. It was loud enough for Dick, and everyone else, to hear. 'You're all the same. All tarred with the same brush.'

She didn't see it coming. The force of it swept her off her feet and she came down, catching her head on the corner of the oven as she landed on the carpet with a heavy thump. Mum leaped out of her chair.

'*Dick!*'

'Come on, darling. Let's get you up,' Aunty Net murmured, for the second time that day.

'Get out,' Mum shouted at Dick Roberts, her face reddening and voice fraying with the effort not to cough. 'I've had it up to here with you... Get out of my house!'

Dick Roberts didn't seem to hear her. He'd completely drained of colour, and he vacillated between bending towards Nan B and backing away.

'Mum? *Don't you touch her.* She's bleeding, you bastard. Mum? Are you all right? Didn't you hear me? I said get out. Get out!'

Aunty Net ducked up and down, fussing ineptly. James had pulled himself up and darted across the room the instant Dick Roberts struck Nan. He grabbed hold of my hand and stood beside me: his tears curtailed, his nose flaring. His eyes were wide and shiny. 'She's dead,' he whispered. 'He's killed her.' But she wasn't, and he hadn't, and we watched together as her fingers emerged, tentatively feeling over the stovetop. She struggled to her feet, rebuffing Aunty Net and Mum's clumsy gestures.

'Get off me. I can't bear a fuss.'

Her white curls bobbed into view, followed by her head. Bright blood coated the right side of her face. It trickled down from a gash, in her temple and coloured the fringes of her hair. A candyfloss cloud smudged and darkened on her lapel.

'I'm all right,' she said.

She avoided Mum and Aunty Net's stunned expressions and stood, flicking distractedly at her coat. Then she raised a hand up to her forehead, and her face clouded.

'Let's sit you down.'

'Mum? Come on, Mum.'

Nan didn't answer. She stood, casually scrutinizing the wet scarlet streaks. She rubbed her finger and thumb together, as if checking the texture of money or the quality of a fine silk sheet. She looked up, frowning at nothing, and didn't resist as Mum put a guiding arm around her shoulders and started to steer her over to one of the chairs. Aunty Net followed them.

'I didn't mean–' Dick Roberts stuttered. 'Katie?'

He took a step forward.

'I didn't...' he floundered and looked confusedly round the rest of the room.

'James...' he said. 'Janet ... Janet?'

He took a step towards me, and raised his hand in some sort of conciliatory gesture. I moved backwards, pressing myself further into the sink. He stopped, looking strangely at me.

'No, no – I'm not going to...'

But it didn't matter. I couldn't help it, I'd started to cry by then: big, messy sobs. Dick Roberts winced.

'What are you doing to her?' Mum shouted. 'Don't you upset her! Get out. Didn't you hear me? *Get out!*'

He didn't need telling again. He turned to cast a final glance at Mum and rushed from the room, treading on the flowers in his hurry.

'Stop crying, you big baby,' James whispered, dropping my hand.

Aunty Net and Mum continued to cluster around Nan. Mum had dampened a J-cloth. She crouched down with it, pressing it into Nan's hair. Nan rustled every now and again, complaining that Mum was making too much of a fuss, but mainly she stayed quiet and let her get on with it. She sat with her eyes closed, her face strangely naked without her glasses, which lay, upside down, on the kitchen table.

'You need a couple of stitches in that.' Aunty Net shuddered, as Mum peeled off the cloth.

Nan only grunted, and waved her off.

After a few minutes Dick Roberts's feet pounded back down the stairs. The front door slammed, and I turned to see him half-walking, half-running up the garden path. He was wearing his black donkey jacket, his head was bowed and he was carrying an old battered suitcase. He stopped, tugging frantically at the garden gate. It finally swung open with its usual high-pitched wail, and it was only then that Mum looked around.

'Dick!' she called, pulling herself up. She hurried over the room, breathing heavily, and pushed past us. 'Where are you going? *Dick!*'

But it was too late. I wiped my eyes, as she banged pointlessly on the window, and looked down at the crushed flower heads, with their weeping trail of scarlet petals. It was too late. He'd already disappeared.

Epilogue

'It's sunny today,' I said, pulling back the net curtains to look out of the bedroom window.

'Yeah, yeah,' James said.

He was on his bunk, lying on his belly with his feet in the air and his chin in his hands, flicking through the latest *Spiderman*. He'd already read it twice, but he still didn't bother to look up.

'Well, it is – even if you don't want to look at it.'

It was a nice morning. I unhooked the latch and pushed open the window, and a soft gust of air hit my face as I leaned out. The sky was a lovely pastel blue. There wasn't a cloud in sight. People were out and about, making the most of it. An elderly couple were wearing their Sunday best and smiling happily as they strolled past: just as if Cumberland Road was some seaside promenade and they were young again. A few solitary figures were walking their dogs. A man sat reading a paper on one of the park benches; a large group of teenagers was playing football at the far end of the field. Occasionally they let out a cheer loud enough for me to hear. Pledgie was nowhere in sight. Neither was Neil. Danny was the only one of that lot I could see. He was standing alone, just outside the entrance of the ditch, prodding the ground with a long stick.

'I can see Danny.'

'So?'

'He's your friend.'

'Not any more, he's not.'

This was news to me. I turned, looking up at James.

'Why not?'

'He's not hard enough.'

'Oh,' I said. I twisted back round, and eyed Danny speculatively. He'd dropped the stick and was crouching down, poking a finger into the long, scraggly grass. Perhaps he'd seen something: a piece of treasure, a murder clue. 'What about Neil and Pledgie?'

'What about them?'

'Are you still friends with them?'

'Yeah, 'course.'

'Oh.'

'Anyway,' James grunted, turning a page, 'I thought you said you were going out.'

'I am.'

'Go on then.'

'You're just annoyed because you're not allowed out.'

'Yeah, yeah. Spaz off.'

He said 'spaz off' with his tongue between his lower gum and lips – so that it came out sounding like he was a spastic – and stuck two fingers up, by way of goodbye. I hesitated, but didn't bother to retaliate. I was getting used to the fact that from now on his insults were always going to be three years older and meaner than mine.

'Spaz off yourself,' was all I said.

I closed the window, and left.

Mum and Nan were in the kitchen. Mum was sat at the table with Nan's pink rollers in her hair while Nan – her own temple decorated with three tiny butterfly stitches – stood beating a Yorkshire pudding mix.

'Don't you give in, Katie,' Nan was saying. She stopped to add another splash of milk to the thick batter. 'If he's coming back here, you need to lay down some ground rules. You've got to let him know who's the boss.'

Mum sighed in response, and ran her fingers through the back of her hair. Her eyes wandered to the cigarette packet lying, half open, on the table beside her.

'And I can tell you now...' Nan paused, straightening up and looking over at Mum to make sure that she was watching before she gave her stitches a meaningful tap. 'He's not getting any sympathy from me. Not after this.'

Mum nodded. She shifted in her seat and averted her eyes, pulling her dressing gown tighter around her middle.

'I know, Mum. But what with this hospital business I've got to think of the kids.'

Nan tutted. 'But you can't spare a thought for your poor mother.'

She went back to her mixing, and after a moment or two gave a little, pointed sniff. But at that same moment Mum glanced round, and saw me hovering in the doorway.

'What are you after?'

'Can I go out?'

She was going to say no, I could tell. I went to turn and go back upstairs, but hesitated when Nan interrupted.

'Don't mollycoddle her, Katie. You're over-protective. No wonder she gets picked on at school.'

'I don't get picked on,' I said.

'Then what do you call that?' Nan asked. She pointed at the fading grazes on my knees, raising her eyebrows. 'Love and affection?'

'Yeah, but ... that was ages ago. We're friends now.'

'Are you, now?' she said. But she smiled faintly, and picked the mixing bowl back up. 'Go on then, while the sun's shining. Bugger off.'

I turned and ran to the front door, ignoring Mum's scowl.

A few cars drove past, different colours: red, blue and the occasional black. Somewhere above me, enfolded in the leaves of the tree, a bird twittered. I sat beneath the Hornet Swatting Tree, scooping out a small hole in the earth around its base. My hands were getting mucky from the dirt, and bits of grit were getting under my nails, but I didn't really mind. It had to be done.

To my right, I could see Aunty Net rummaging around in her front garden. She held a black sack in one hand; she was wearing a pair of yellow marigolds, and was clearing away the mounds of rubbish that had built over time and cluttered up either side of her garden path. I hadn't seen her for over a week, not since Dick Roberts had left and she'd disappeared from ours in a huff, after Nan had recovered enough to get up and pour Aunty Net's bottle of vodka down the sink. She was wearing a headscarf now, just like Mum did when she did her spring-cleans. She'd waved when she saw me walking down the road, but hadn't called me over. I'd never seen Aunty Net tidying, ever.

I straightened up, and smoothed the rumpled square in my hand. It was the picture of the Killer, the one from the *Oxford Mail*.

'What are you doing?'

I looked up. It was Danny, standing over me. He readjusted his glasses and squinted, looking down at the picture. I turned it over quickly, so he couldn't see.

'I've been watching you,' he said. 'You've been digging a hole for the past ten minutes. What's it for?'

'Why should I tell you?'

He put his hands in his pockets and backed away, blushing slightly and shrugging. I looked at him, biting my lip.

'I'll go then,' he said.

A ray of sun filtered through the leaves of the tree, catching and warming my cheeks.

'No, don't go,' I said. I picked up the square of paper, and gave him a quick glimpse of the portrait before I hid it in the folds of my skirt again. 'It's for this. I'm burying it.'

'Why?'

I hesitated.

'Who is it?'

'It's…'

I trailed off, looking over to the sports field railings – the bit just outside the ditch. A fresh bunch of pink flowers had been tied there. Danny swung his foot over the ground, waiting for an answer. I shrugged, looking down at the portrait, wondering vaguely what Amber Jenkins's mum was doing. She must have been doing something, she was only round the corner – and after all, she did have three other kids that needed looking after.

The newspaper face looked a bit strange, somehow, now that I looked at it: not quite there. It was just an amalgamation of criss-crossed black lines, printed on cheap paper that was already beginning to yellow.

'I don't know,' I said, in the end. 'It's just a piece of paper, I suppose.'

I went to throw it away as I said it but Danny leaned down, and took it off me. I watched him. He folded it over and over, until it was a neat, chubby square, and placed it in the hole I'd made.

'No – it must be someone,' he said. He rubbed his hands together and looked at me. 'Go on then, you first.'

I hesitated for a moment before I realized what he meant. Then I leaned forward on all fours, and gathered a handful of dirt. Danny knelt over me, his palms pressed together, just like people did when they prayed.

'Ashes to ashes,' he began. 'Dust to dust...'

As so it carried on, and with his intonations and my handfuls of dust, I said my farewell to the Killer, and to the last hours of summer.

'I used to call this the Squirrel Tree,' he said, wiping his hands on his trousers and sitting back up.

'Why?'

'Because a squirrel used to live in it.'

'I used to call it the Hornet Swatting Tree.'

'Why?'

'Because there used to be a hornets' nest in it, and we used to swat all the hornets.'

He wrinkled his nose.

'Hornets can kill you, you know.'

'So?'

We sat for a while, looking at the little brown mound.

I reached forward, giving it a final pat.

'If it's a burial,' Danny offered, 'we should make a headstone. We can make a cross out of some twigs.'

He picked up a couple and joined them together, showing me.

'Like this.'

I shook my head. He shrugged, and was quiet for a moment.

'Do you want to see the squirrel's old house?'

'Is it still there?'

'I think so. A squirrel's house is called a drey, you know.'

I clambered up, brushing the dust off my legs. My dress was a bit dirty – it was my best one as well. Mum had made me put it on, ready for Dick Roberts and Sunday lunch. It would be the first time he'd been round, since a week last Friday when he'd left, and she wanted to make sure that we made a good impression. He'd been on the phone to Mum – they'd had long conversations that seemed to take up half the night – and Mum had asked me whether I missed him a couple of times, but that was it. I hadn't known what to say when she'd asked me that. She got more out of James, though he can't have given the right answer, because when he said, 'No,' she'd cuffed him round the head and looked put out. I kept quiet, because I didn't want to upset her.

'What do you reckon?' Danny asked.

'I dunno,' I said.

I looked up at the tree, and then down at my legs. I'd be dead if I got into any more of a mess. There were brown smears on my socks and one of my knees had started to bleed a bit, from where a small piece of scab had scratched off when I was kneeling.

'Go on. It'll be good, I swear.'

I looked at him, holding my arm over my eyes to block out the sun. I thought of all the things Mum would have to say when she saw the state of me, later. But ... a real squirrel's nest. A drey.

'All right,' I said.

Out of the corner of my eye I could see that Aunty Net had stopped clearing up and was sitting on the wall with Ann, her next door neighbour. They were laughing about something. She saw me looking, and gave another wave. I waved back. Then I grinned at Danny and turned, looking for a good foothold in the tree base.

'Come on then,' I said. 'Let's go.'

This Large Print Book, for people
who cannot read normal print,
is published under the auspices of

THE ULVERSCROFT FOUNDATION